Just a Cowboy's Shotgun Wedding

Flyboys of Sweet Briar Ranch in North Dakota
Book Seven
Jessie Gussman

Published By: Jessie Gussman

Contents

Acknowledgments

Cover art by Julia Gussman
Editing by Heather Hayden
Narration by Jay Dyess
Author Services by CE Author Assistant

Listen to a FREE professionally performed and produced audiobook version of this title on Youtube. Search for "Say With Jay" to browse all available FREE Dyess/Gussman audiobooks.

Chapter 1

"**M**ommy, Henry hit me."

"I did not! I was just swinging my arm and she got in the way."

"I'm hungry."

"Luna knocked down my block tower. Make her put it back up!"

Piper held a hand to her throbbing head and listened to the chaos of her children around her.

This was what happened when she didn't go to church. It served her right. When she rolled over in the morning and couldn't find the energy to get herself, let alone her six kids, up and ready, it always came back to bite her.

Plus, she missed the fellowship.

As a single mom who worked as hard as she could as a hairdresser, it was nice to get out and hear the Word.

She hadn't even gotten her coffee yet but had been going from crisis to crisis since she'd gotten out of bed.

Spilled milk, spilled cereal, a leaking diaper, a broken lamp, three wrestling matches, two head bumps, three Band-Aids, and that was just hitting the highlights.

The cries of her children didn't diminish as she stood at the stove, pouring pasta into the boiling water and trying to plan a grocery list in her head for the week.

Sunday afternoons were a terrible time to go grocery shopping, but she was booked solid with hairdressing clients Monday, Tuesday, and Wednesday.

On Wednesday, their area of North Dakota was supposed to get a big storm. People had been calling and canceling, shifting their appointments either earlier or later.

She needed to have groceries so she could ride out the storm, too.

The problem was, she needed money to buy groceries. She'd only had enough to get the absolute necessities last Thursday.

The extra bookings on the first three days of the week would be good for her pocketbook, although the lack of customers at the end of the week would more than make up for the abundance, she was sure.

"Ingrid," she said to her six-year-old, "Henry is spinning around in a circle. He's dizzy and can't control where he's going. Stand back away from him so he doesn't hit you."

She reached down and patted the top of her daughter's head as she clung to her leg, crying.

There were no red marks on her face and no new bumps that she could see. Ingrid had a tendency to be a bit dramatic.

Probably because she was a middle child who longed for attention.

The thought made Piper feel guilty. Was she not giving her kids enough attention?

She'd been assured by the ladies at church that it was perfectly normal for kids to want more attention than what their parents gave them. That middle children often developed ways of garnering attention for themselves, and it had nothing to do with Piper's lack of parenting skills.

She wanted to believe that, but it was hard.

Setting the empty box of pasta on the counter, she didn't stir it but knelt down, putting both arms around Ingrid.

"I think you're going to be okay. You can't cry every time someone touches you. Even if it hurts, a lot of times you have to just let it go. Especially if you know that you can go somewhere else in order to avoid being hit."

She hadn't been watching, didn't know for sure that Henry hadn't meant to hit Ingrid. But Ingrid was two years older than Henry was, and she was perfectly capable of getting out of his way.

"I'm hungry," Luna said beside her.

At two, almost three, Luna had really started to talk, and her favorite two words were "I'm hungry."

Theodora, who was almost two and who still hadn't grown enough hair to make her actually look like a girl so most people mistook her for a little boy, toddled over, seeing her mom kneeling down and wanting her fair share of attention, too.

Without really planning it, Piper ended up sitting on the floor, Ingrid on her lap, Luna and Theodora pushing in on either side, while Henry came running in, wanting to know where all of his playmates were, with Alice trailing behind.

It made for a lot of chaos in the kitchen, since the only one of her children who wasn't there was nine-year-old Lucas.

Sometimes she thought Lucas appreciated school just because he got to leave the chaos of his home and go someplace where things were a little more structured and calm.

That didn't mean that Lucas didn't love them or that he wouldn't do everything in his power to help his mom.

He was far too serious, since the death of her husband, almost two years ago.

Theodora had never met her father, since Piper had been pregnant with her at the time.

If she kept thinking about her late husband, she'd end up not only on the floor with all the kids on top of her, but crying as well.

"Guys, I need to stir the pasta. Or we won't have any lunch. It will all be stuck in a big goopy pile at the bottom of the pan."

Her kids didn't understand, at least Luna and Theodora didn't, and Ingrid still clung tightly to her neck.

She should have just shut the water off and planned on sitting on the floor and holding her kids for a little bit.

She had to work so much that she often didn't spend as much time with her kids as she wanted to.

She never scheduled clients on Sundays, and usually they went to church, when she could get herself dragged out of bed and get her kids ready in time.

Her husband, Richard, would have wanted her to take them.

She wanted to, too, just sometimes her want-tos didn't always equal her able-tos.

They sat like that until the water boiled over and started hissing on the stove.

The sound was enough to startle her children, which enabled her to scramble up, turning the heat down and grabbing a spoon to stir the sticking pasta.

It would be gluey but edible.

As she was setting the spoon down, she saw her phone light up with a text. She almost let it go, until a time with less chaos around her, but there really was never a time with less chaos, plus the fact that the storm was coming, and that a lot of clients were rescheduling, made her grab it and look.

> If it's okay with you, I'm going to come out this afternoon and get started on the addition.

She didn't recognize the number, but she didn't need to once she read the message. It was Gideon Marsh.

The chaos of her children playing wasn't quite as loud as it had been before she spent a few minutes on the floor with her kids, and her mind wandered as she walked to the cupboard and pulled out a jar of spaghetti sauce.

Gideon was coming.

She'd been hearing all last fall that he'd be coming to help put an addition onto her house. One she sorely needed, since she had her children divided into two bedrooms while she slept on the couch.

Before Richard died, he had been planning on adding on, but he intended to do most of the work himself and had been planning on taking on some extra jobs in order to pay for the lumber and materials.

Of course, after his death, that hadn't been something that was going to happen. Except the townspeople had rallied together and bought the materials.

Gideon had been supposed to do it last fall, but he had broken his leg and it had taken all winter to heal.

She assumed, since it was late March, that he would be starting whatever it was that he did with his friends on Sweet Briar Ranch soon. She knew they ran a crop-dusting service, plus she'd recently heard they were working on getting a dude ranch up. One of the perks of being a hairdresser was that she usually stayed up on all the local town news.

It seemed like the ex-Air Force dudes out on Sweet Briar Ranch were always busy with something, and she felt terrible that Mr. Marsh, *Gideon*, was going to be taking time off to come put on her addition. Although, listening to the chaos in her kitchen and thinking about how nice it would be to have a little bit more space, she looked forward to it.

She appreciated it, truly.

Except...she didn't like the way she felt like she owed people who gave things to her, and if he spent most of the spring putting an addition on her house, she would owe him more than she could ever repay.

The ladies at church had told her over and over again that the Lord would take care of him and the Lord would eventually enable her to pass it on, but it still made her uncomfortable.

She'd never been someone who had needed charity before. And it didn't sit well with her.

It was her pride, she knew that.

Setting the jar of pasta sauce down and picking her phone back up, she sent a simple text.

Okay.

She wasn't going to fight, she wasn't going to argue, and she was going to try as hard as she could to be grateful.

His text came back right away.

Is one o'clock okay?

She glanced at the clock. 12:30. The kids would be done eating, easily. It didn't take them long at all. She might not have the mess cleaned up, but it didn't matter. The house was a disaster, with toys everywhere, blankets and pillows scattered around. The glass from the broken lamp had been cleaned up, but she'd moved the furniture out and not moved it back. The floor needed to be swept, and there was a huge stack of dishes in the sink.

She'd had clients until ten o'clock last night and hadn't done dishes for three days.

He might as well get to see what her house was going to typically look like while he was there.

It was just a pride thing that made her want to make it look different than it usually did.

Or maybe she wanted to put her best foot forward.

Not that she thought there was any chance of anything other than a very loose friendship between her and Gideon. It was just the idea that she didn't want to be pitied any more than she already was.

Maybe he wouldn't even notice the dirty house. Richard never had. He'd walked across her clean kitchen floor with mud on his shoes and never noticed that he was tracking it everywhere.

It irritated her, but it wasn't hard to forgive, or even overlook, because he had been such a good man. A good husband, a good father, but of course he wasn't perfect. She didn't expect him to be and wasn't going to complain about something simple like that, when he did so many other things exactly right.

Her heart gave a little squeeze at the thought, and she again pushed thoughts of Richard out of her head.

They had started dating about this time of year, and she supposed it was only natural that she thought about him a little more than what she normally did.

Grabbing her phone, she typed out one word.

Yes.

Chapter 2

Gideon Marsh pulled into the drive, parking his pickup beside an SUV that looked like it was at least twenty years old.

He was here to put an addition on her home, but it looked like her car could use some work too.

His friend, Baker, could help with that.

He made a mental note to ask.

He stopped with his hand on the door handle when movement caught his eye. He squinted through the windshield.

Was that a...cow?

It looked like the steer that ran loose through Sweet Water.

He got out of the pickup a little more slowly than he had intended, all the while trying to get a better glimpse of the cow which stood, partially hidden by an old shed at the side of Piper's property.

He was almost positive that was Billy the steer who chased Munchy the pig around through Sweet Water.

Piper lived just a few minutes outside of town, but it seemed like an awful long way for the steer to navigate.

Of course, he didn't know much about cattle, since he and his buddies just had a few, and he'd only been working with them for a couple of years.

Maybe cattle did naturally move around a lot if they weren't fenced in.

Regardless, the steer had always been good with kids. He'd seen him several times at different festivals in Sweet Water, with kids climbing all over him, and he had seemed perfectly calm and almost like he enjoyed the attention.

Of course, with Piper having six children, maybe Billy had found his niche.

It really shouldn't matter to Gideon. He was only going to be here for a month or two at most, to put the addition up.

Depending on how much time he had to work, he might be able to get it finished earlier.

Leaving his toolbox in the truck for the time being, he walked to the front door. She should be expecting him, since he'd texted her and, he looked at his watch, he was right on time.

He made it up the steps to the porch when the door flew open and three or four kids came running out in various stages of dress. Or undress, depending on one's modesty preferences.

Gideon hid a grin. More than once, his friends had accused him of being a big kid. He loved to laugh and joke and goof off. Although, he believed as he got older he had been better at shouldering the responsibilities of adulthood, and when it came to building or working, his dad had seen to it that he had drilled into his head the importance of doing good work.

But beyond that, he loved to play and just be a big kid, and he'd always loved children.

He'd just never been able to get any woman to take a chance on him long enough to get married and have any.

He had more than one ex-girlfriend who called him immature.

Hopefully, it wasn't because he was selfish or self-centered, but just because he enjoyed messing around, and the idea of getting serious with romance always made him squirm.

He'd quit trying for the last few years, ever since Erin. He had been as serious about her as he could be about anyone, as she almost seemed like she was going to be able to put up with him. Almost.

Shoving the thought out of his head, he grinned at the kids who came tumbling out the door. They froze as they stared at him.

He'd been looking forward to this job, not just because he enjoyed building things, and hadn't been able to for a while, but because of all the kids. Surely there would be downtime where he'd get to play with them, and maybe they'd even be interested in helping him. They'd definitely provide variety and interest on this job.

His eyes lifted as a shadow filled the door, and his gaze landed on Piper.

For having six kids, she looked young. Slender. But, oh, so tired. He felt bad for her. He couldn't imagine anyone looking at her and not feeling that way, if they knew of her situation. Having lost her husband when she was pregnant with her sixth child. Ever since then struggling to make ends meet.

His heart went out to her, and he knew he was making the right decision to do this for her for free, just because of the way he felt inside.

It would make anyone feel good helping someone out, doing a good deed, giving something of themselves to be a blessing to someone else.

"Thanks for coming out, Gideon," she said above the clamor of her kids as the wind gusted across the porch, stirring dried corn leaves and grass.

The littlest one on the porch turned back to their mom and put her hands up, silently begging to be picked up.

As Piper lifted her onto her hip, he said, "My pleasure, ma'am."

He felt like he should tip his hat, but that seemed like overkill and a little bit of a formality that seemed out of place on a porch where one child wore nothing but a diaper and one had red stuff that he guessed might be spaghetti or tomato sauce all over his face.

The old T-shirt, thin, with the hem unraveling, and the worn blue jeans that Piper wore added to the general feeling of disarray.

Not to mention the porch was small, and he suddenly felt cramped.

Maybe it was the look in her eye. A look that said she was grateful but not super happy.

He wasn't sure where he got that idea, but it allowed some of the air to leak out of his happy bubble. Where was the fun in doing something for someone who didn't want you there?

"Am I coming at a bad time?" he asked, hearing the hesitation in his voice.

"No," Piper said with a ghost of a smile which tilted her lips up just a little, like she found his question funny.

Maybe every time was a bad time. He wasn't sure. While he loved kids and had never truly outgrown his own childhood, he hadn't been around them that much.

"If you want to follow me, I'll take you back."

"I can walk around the house so I don't drag any dirt in," he offered, just in case it was the idea of a strange man in her house that had made that shadow cross her face.

"You can't make it any dirtier than what it already is," she said softly, shaking her head as she turned and led the way into the house.

Two of the kids walked in in front of him, while the oldest one, at least the tallest one, a boy, held the door open for him.

He nodded his head at the kid.

"My name's Gideon," he said. At the last moment, he held his hand out, unsure whether the kid would even know what to do with it.

The boy looked at his hand, then back up into his face, then back down at his hand.

Maybe it was Gideon's imagination, but the thin chest seemed to puff out a little as the boy's hand came out and clasped Gideon's.

"I'm Lucas. I'm nine."

"Wow. Nine," Gideon said, wondering if he should have offered his own age when he offered his name.

"Yep. And I'm big enough to help. Mom said I could if you said it was okay."

"That's funny. As I was driving over here, I was thinking to myself that it'd be real nice if I had someone to give me a hand. You're hired."

"I'm *hired*?" Lucas said, his voice going up an octave, in surprise and disbelief.

"Sure are. Although, I guess your pay will depend on your dedication and willingness to work."

"You mean you're really going to pay me?"

Gideon smiled at the boy's enthusiasm, but it also made his throat tighten some, that the kid would be so excited about...attention? Money? Being given a job and having a purpose?

He wasn't sure exactly what it was that had Lucas grinning like a cat lapping cream, but he was happy that he'd been able to put that expression on his face.

"Sure am. As long as you do a good job and you're not afraid to work."

"Mom says I do the dishes really well. She said maybe next year I could mow the grass by myself."

Gideon grinned. By the time he was Lucas's age, nine, he had been mowing the grass by himself for years. His dad hadn't believed in waiting just because Gideon hadn't been tall enough for his feet to reach the pedals on their riding lawnmower. That didn't make any difference to him. His dad had strapped wooden blocks onto them, and that solved that problem.

Some people might be upset about that, but Gideon had loved it, and he credited his dad with helping him to build a good work ethic from a very young age.

Chapter 3

"Lucas, don't bother Mr. Gideon. He's here to work."

Piper's voice didn't hold anger or censure, but she clearly meant what she said. Lucas closed his mouth and looked down.

"It's okay. Unless there's a reason you don't want him to talk to me. I really like kids. Always have. Maybe that's because I'm just a big kid myself. At least that's what people say."

He'd been accused of that all of his life. He'd actually worked hard on trying to be a little more mature, less likely to do something stupid, but he still loved goofing off.

"I just don't want him to bother you. A lot of people don't like to have kids running around while they're trying to work," she said, with apology and concern in her voice.

"I promise if there's a problem, I'll say so, but I actually like the chaos. Noise drives some people crazy, but not me."

She lifted her brows, almost as though his words surprised her. But if she knew his personality at all, they really shouldn't.

Maybe she didn't know. They went to the same church but hardly ever, if ever, spoke to each other. He didn't exactly hang out wherever she did. Which was probably wherever the kids of the church were.

Since he'd moved to Sweet Water a few years ago, her attendance had been sporadic. He'd heard people attribute that to the fact that her husband had passed away and she had all the kids to take care of by herself.

It did seem like kids were a lot of fun, but he supposed they were a lot of work as well. Not that he would know, since he'd never had the responsibility of watching even one, let alone six.

There was a part of him, a part that was bigger than he maybe wanted to admit, that thought having six kids would make everything more fun.

Not that he actually wanted to have six kids of his own. He didn't. Only crazy people did that.

He stopped that thought before it went any further. He didn't want to insult Piper. But that did seem to be the general consensus in the world today. That one or two kids was okay, three was pushing it, and any more was irresponsible.

He wasn't sure he agreed with that, but it wasn't like he had to think about it overmuch, either.

Piper had nodded her head, then turned around to continue walking, leading him toward the area where he'd be working.

Maybe if she hadn't been turned around, maybe if he hadn't distracted her, or if there weren't so many kids yelling and making noise, or maybe if she hadn't been holding the baby on one hip, Gideon wasn't sure, but he thought that she would have seen the toy tractor lying on the floor and would have been able to avoid stepping on it.

As it was, it seemed to happen in slow motion before him. Slow motion, but too fast for him to run ahead and grab her, as her foot went out from underneath her, twisting on the way down, as she started to fall, but throwing herself to the side so she wasn't falling on the baby she had on her hip.

He noticed that and was impressed by it, even as he ran toward her, getting there just as she hit the ground.

"If this were a romance novel, I would have caught you." He wasn't sure why those words came out of his mouth. He should utter some kind words of compassion or ask if she was okay, but it probably had to do with the reason everyone told him he was immature.

He never had quite the right words to say and ended up saying something that totally didn't fit the situation.

Immediately he said, "I'm sorry. Are you okay?" He spoke in a loud tone beside her, through the cries of her children and the crying of the baby, who had landed on her hip and was fine, just surprised.

Gideon's hand landed on her shoulder. She didn't answer right away, and as Gideon looked closer, her face was pulled up in a grimace. He figured that maybe the twist he saw her do had put more pressure on her ankle than he had first thought.

He waited, knowing from experience that when he first got hurt, the sharp pain needed to fade before he could talk to anyone.

Unsure if the child would let him pick her up, he reached out to get her off her hip.

For him, when he was dealing with the initial, acute throbbing, he was a lot more sensitive to anything that touched him. He couldn't imagine having a child jumping on him.

"Hey there, let me hold you," he said easily and softly as he picked the kid up. She was wearing pink, but the hair was a boy cut.

Or maybe the child just hadn't grown hair out. He wasn't sure.

Surely the mom wouldn't dress a boy in pink? Back when he was a kid, he would have said no way, but in today's world, he supposed a person couldn't tell the gender just by looking at the colors the child wore.

"That's Theodora," the tallest girl said from beside his elbow.

"Thanks," he said, grateful that she come over. As he'd been looking, the baby's face had started to scrunch up, but when she saw her sister, it smoothed out. Not completely, but enough that he didn't think she was going to erupt into a yell imminently.

"She doesn't let anyone but Mom hold her," the other little girl said matter-of-factly.

"Well, your mom isn't able to right now, so hopefully Theodora won't mind if I substitute for a bit."

The baby wasn't going to have a choice, so he did his best to look nonthreatening, whatever that looked like, as his gaze shifted back to Piper.

She had been pushing herself up off the floor, but as his eyes skimmed down her legs, he could tell from the angle of her foot that whatever she'd done to it, it was going to take an emergency room visit to fix it.

"Do you have someone I can call? I'm pretty sure that's broken, and we're going to need to make a trip to Rockerton." He didn't mean to be bossy. Usually, he was much more easygoing, and he didn't even realize he was commanding her until her brows rose and her eyes widened when he used the word "we."

She took a deep breath, but it was shaky, and he figured that maybe if all the kids hadn't been around, she would be crying.

He couldn't guarantee that he wouldn't be, looking at the way she held her foot. He grimaced then averted his eyes. Blood and breaks were not his thing. Whether he had been in the Air Force or not, it didn't matter. His specialty had been working on broken airplanes. Not broken humans. And despite the fact that he'd been in a hostage situation, he never actually had to shoot anyone, thankfully, during his time in the service.

Plus, he'd just broken his leg last fall when he fell on some ice, and seeing Piper made the painful feeling come right back.

"I want to argue with you, but I think you might be right." Her voice was low. He still heard it over the chatter of the kids around them and the oblivious playing of what looked like a two-year-old and maybe a four-year-old.

Lucas stood beside his mom, his hands clasped in front of him, his lips pulled into his mouth, and his face scrunched up in a worried look.

"I could call my buddies, and I know they'd come. But your kids might feel more comfortable with someone else?" he prompted her. He didn't want her to be in pain any longer than she had to be. Interesting, because he wanted to scoop her up and carry her directly out to his truck, but they needed to do something with the kids. Not a complication he was used to having to deal with.

This was one of those things that kids made more difficult. His eyes had been opened just a little to that, since he had never considered a situation like this involving kids before.

"Do you have Miss April's phone number?" she asked, the words seeming to be pulled out of her, like she was trying to speak without putting all the pain she felt into her voice.

"I do. I'll call right away."

"I can hold Theodora," the girl who had told him Theodora's name said.

"Thanks. What's your name?" he asked, figuring that it probably wouldn't hurt to get to know the kids. Piper might be down now, but that wouldn't affect whether or not he put an addition onto her house.

It might affect whether or not she could work.

His hands stopped for just a second at that thought.

He didn't know what her situation was. Not being able to work would be a problem for anyone, but for a single mom who was depending on herself to take care of her family, it could be devastating.

That wasn't the bridge they had to cross tonight though, so he pushed the thought out of his head and handed Theodora over to the little girl who said her name was Alice before he pulled his phone out of his pocket.

"Thanks, Alice, although I'm pretty sure Theodora was okay with me holding her." He had to rub it in a little. After all, Theodora had wrapped her arms around his neck and hadn't wanted to let go when Alice took her from him.

"She never likes anyone. I don't know why she likes you. Maybe she was just scared because Mom fell."

"That could be. But she obviously loves you too." He smiled up at Alice, who gave him a serious smile back. She looked like a little mother, so sweet holding her sister, with Theodora's chubby arms wrapped around her little neck.

He looked down at his phone and pulled up Miss April's number easily.

It rang twice before she answered.

"Hello?"

"Miss April. It's Gideon Marsh."

"I know. Your name came up on my phone."

He was never sure. Half the time, he didn't take the time to program people's names into his phone, and he had no idea who was calling him. He supposed a more responsible person, like Miss April, made sure that names got programmed in.

"Right. So I was out here looking at Piper's house, and she fell. I think she's broken her ankle or her foot or something. She needs to go to Rockerton to the ER. I can take her, but someone needs to come out and watch the kids. She suggested you. Would you be able to do it?"

His gaze had landed on Piper, who looked very pale to him and lay on the floor with her eyes closed. She hadn't even tried to get up again.

Her three older children, with Alice holding Theodora, stood over her, watching while the other two continued to play. He kept an eye on them, making sure they didn't run into her foot. He could imagine how bad it must hurt, but having a kid fall on it would make it feel even worse.

"I'll be right out," Miss April said, without asking for any more details.

"All right. We'll wait until you get here, but I might have her in the truck. She's in a lot of pain."

At that, her eyes opened, and she waited for him to hang up before she said, "How do you know? I didn't say that."

"You didn't have to. I can see it around your eyes, and I don't want you to worry, but you're a lot more pale than I'm comfortable with. How are you feeling?" he asked, wishing he'd paid more attention in his first-aid classes.

What constituted a person going into shock? He was pretty sure paleness was one of the signs. Was their skin supposed to be clammy?

He reached out to touch her and only hesitated a moment when she flinched, then uttered an apology.

"I should have told you what I was doing. I wanted to see if your skin was clammy."

"That's fine. I just saw something coming, and even though it's not anywhere near my foot, I wanted to get out of the way." There was a little bit of laughter mixed in with the pain in her voice, and he smiled along with her.

"I can't blame you for that at all." Their eyes met, and despite the cloudy pain in hers, he felt some kind of connection.

Maybe it was the idea that pain united them. Even though he wasn't feeling it now, he understood the sharp pain of a break and the need to put on a brave front. Maybe he hadn't done it for his children, but he'd done it when his buddies were standing around.

Regardless, he felt a connection with her that, up until that point, he hadn't. He'd felt bad for her, because of her situation, of her losing her husband and having so many children depend on her, where she'd obviously been struggling to work as hard as she could to do what she could to provide for them. She looked tired and beaten down, and it pulled at his heartstrings.

But this was different. This was seeing her as an equal, not someone he could help, but someone who understood, and had been through, or was going through, the exact same things he had. Someone he related to. It was an odd feeling, especially considering it was with a woman like Piper. Someone he really didn't have much of anything in common with.

He wasn't married, didn't have kids, and was pretty much free to do whatever he wanted to do. She was the exact opposite and looked like someone who was more serious, less prone to taking risks, and just generally his opposite in every way.

It was odd. But he didn't question it too much, just enjoyed the fact that they had found something in common. Even if it was something like pain.

"Is there anything you need me to do to get ready for Miss April coming?" he asked, although what he really wanted to ask her was if he could get her off the floor, pick her up and put her on the couch. But after the way she flinched when he had tried to touch her face, he thought that maybe he ought to just leave well enough alone.

He was going to have to pick her up eventually, because there was no way she was going to hobble out to his truck. Jumping with her foot, if it was broken, would jar it and make the pain a hundred times worse.

She closed her eyes and sighed, tiredness and pain mixing in the exhale. "No. Whatever she does will be fine."

He almost laughed. He didn't visit his sister much, but when he did, they had a two-page list of things that they wanted to have done with their only child when they left, which was not very often and was not ever in Gideon's care. He hadn't had to worry about following the list but had felt pity for the person who had come and had been confronted with all the different things that his sister expected out of someone who watched her precious baby.

Gideon wasn't entirely sure that a child who was so coddled would turn out any better than six kids who weren't, but there was no doubt in his mind that his sister was doing the very best that she could, whether that was coddling her kid or not, and he wouldn't fight with her about it.

"Lucas, you're going to need to make sure to get Henry and Luna's jammies. Alice, you can take care of Theodora, make sure that Miss April knows where diapers are. You know where the Cheerios are and her crackers."

Lucas and Alice nodded solemnly at their mother.

"Ingrid." Piper took a moment to make eye contact with this serious-looking little girl who stood staring down at her mom, tears pooling in her eyes. "Don't cry. Mom is going to be fine. I'll probably come back with a really fun cast on my foot, and you'll get to put your names on it. It's going to be a lot of fun. Just as soon as it stops hurting, which it will when I get to the hospital, okay?"

Her voice had lowered, and there was kindness and compassion in it. She seemed to know that the little girl who stared at her, trying so bravely to keep her tears from falling, needed a little extra attention.

"I need you to be a big girl and take care of yourself, okay?"

Ingrid's head went up and down, but she didn't say anything.

"And do you remember how you cooked scrambled eggs for everyone last week for breakfast?" she asked in a gentle tone that Gideon had to admire considering the pain she must be in.

Ingrid nodded again.

"Do you think you could do that for supper tonight?"

Ingrid's lips quirked up, and her chest puffed out just a bit. She nodded, a little faster than she had before, as though she were excited that she would be able to cook and do something to help while her mom was not feeling well.

Gideon figured that the warm, achy feeling in his chest was something the world would term love, but the little girl was just so sweetly brave that he couldn't keep the feeling from expanding his chest and turning his own lips up. What a cutie.

"I'll tell Miss April that you're going to do that."

Ingrid nodded, and then she whispered, so softly that Gideon had to strain to hear, "Should I start now?"

"Yes. Why don't you go ahead and do that," Piper said, giving Ingrid a look like she had just taken the world off her shoulders.

Gideon suspected that Piper wanted her to volunteer to go so that she wouldn't be standing there watching as Piper grimaced and dealt with the pain.

"Come on, Alice, let's you and me get the little kids ready for their naps." Lucas, casting a worried glance at his mother and probably figuring out what Gideon had just figured out, that Piper was trying to get the kids away from her so it wouldn't upset them to see her, decided to help.

"Do you want me to pick you up and set you on the couch?" Gideon said as the children walked slowly away, as though they were reluctant to leave their mother lying on the floor.

Piper sighed. Then she smiled a little and huffed out a bit of a laugh. "I'm such a coward. I would much rather greet Miss April from the couch, but I'm scared to death that you're going to pick me up and it's going to hurt. The sharp, almost unbearable pain has settled into a throbbing that I can pretty much handle, but I'm afraid if I get jiggled, it's going to be that unbearable pain again." She gave him an abashed look. "Sorry. I told you I was a coward."

"No. You're not. That kind of pain is hard for anyone. I've seen grown men howling in agony over a break just like this. No one blames you for not wanting to increase your pain."

"I don't want my children's main memory of their childhood to be their mother lying on the floor screaming in pain. Something like that they couldn't possibly forget."

"I have to agree with that. I never saw my mom do that, but I'm sure I wouldn't have forgotten it if I had."

She nodded. And he had to admire her for thinking about it. For knowing what would be best for her children and, even in her pain, doing the best she could for them.

He'd seen so many mothers who didn't care that much about their kids at all. Not nearly enough to want to keep them from experiencing trauma if they could help it. Just living for themselves and doing whatever was best for them.

She closed her eyes, like the words themselves were painful. "But if you're willing, I think that would be best. I'll sound like I have more authority if I'm sitting on the couch. And I love Miss April, but she can have a tendency to be a little pushy."

Gideon grunted, trying to contain his laughter. That was true. He had more than one conversation with Miss April in church where he felt like he'd been bulldozed into doing something he hadn't really been the slightest bit interested in doing but had been herded into it against his will.

Chapter 4

"All right. I'm going to put my hands under your knees and under your back. You put your arms around my neck, and I will try as hard as I can to not jiggle your foot as I'm standing."

Gideon's heart started to thump, and his hands sweat. He didn't want to laugh, but it seemed humorous, with all the things that he'd done in his life, that this, picking this woman up, afraid to cause her more pain, would make him nervous.

"And just in my defense, and so you have full disclosure, I've never done this before, so I'm not entirely sure that I'm going to be able to do it, or that I'll do it successfully, and worst-case scenario, I'll drop you and land on top of you. Should I have you sign a waiver?"

He was mostly joking, just wanting to lighten the mood or maybe ease his nerves by laughing, but she giggled, and he figured that he helped her as much as he helped himself.

He appreciated that bit of laughter, and as he was slipping his arms under her legs and around her back, he thought of his ex-fiancée, Erin. The only woman he'd ever been really serious about. She would have been upset at him joking at such a serious time. She would have reprimanded him and told him that he needed to grow up.

Of course, she had told him on a daily basis, sometimes several times a day, that he needed to grow up.

Eventually he asked her what in the world she was doing with him, when she thought that he needed to grow up so much.

She hadn't had an answer, and that had been the beginning of the end. Maybe that question had started her thinking and had caused her to decide that she was better off with someone else.

Last he'd heard, she'd been dating a lawyer. That should be sufficiently boring and serious enough for her.

He hadn't tried to keep up with her, just saw her occasionally on social media. And he was truly happy for her. If she wanted a lawyer, someone like Gideon was never going to work for her.

Funny that he'd be thinking about Erin now as he picked up Piper.

Maybe it was that look they'd shared earlier, the one that made him feel like someone actually understood him. At least a part of him. He hadn't even realized he was looking for that, someone to understand him. But the feeling had been so real, so strong, and felt so...right. Good. That someone else could see him and know the things about him that he didn't just tell to anyone, and like him anyway.

He didn't want to keep going down that thought trail, so he focused on making sure he didn't lose his balance and fall forward.

He eyed the far wall; if he did lose his balance, he might be able to use his head to catch himself on the wall so he didn't actually drop her. But that would almost assuredly jar her foot and cause her pain. Something he wanted to avoid if at all possible.

"Are you ready?" he asked, as much for his benefit as for hers.

"I trust you," she said, and while he heard the pain in her voice, there was also a peace there, a confidence he wasn't sure he deserved.

Regardless, he put all of his focus into carefully lifting her and adjusting her in his arms. Lifting her smoothly, jarring her as little as possible.

As he turned, the front door opened, and Miss April stepped in.

If he hadn't called Miss April, told her about Piper's foot and that they needed to go to the ER, he might have been a little embarrassed to have her walking in, seeing them in that exact position, him holding Piper and her arms wrapped around his neck, clinging tightly, probably as much because of the pain as because she needed to.

Miss April's eyes went from his arms around her, to Piper's around his neck, then ran down Piper's body. When they came to her foot and ankle, her eyes widened, and her brows went way up.

"Oh my goodness. That's already swollen to twice its normal size. You guys need to get out of here. Get that girl to the hospital. I'm sure she'd like to get some pain meds as soon as she can."

"She needs pain meds, and for some reason, my foot is starting to hurt too. Probably sympathetic pain. Will pain meds work on that? I'll take some of the good stuff."

Piper giggled again, and he saw that as a good sign, although her hold around his neck didn't loosen. Still, the giggling hopefully meant that he was relieving her mind a little of the pain. He also read somewhere that laughter made pain hurt less, although he couldn't remember where and wasn't sure that was entirely true.

"Why don't you two just head straight out. In fact, I'll go out and open the passenger side door. I assume you're taking her in your truck?" Miss April said, all business.

"I was." He looked down, to see if Piper agreed or not.

Her face was even more pale than it had been, and her lips pressed together.

He assumed, as much as he'd tried not to jiggle her, he hadn't been completely successful.

Since Piper seemed to be focused on not making any noise that showed how much pain she was in, Gideon figured he could speak for her.

"She gave the kids jobs to do. Ingrid—" He thought that was the right name, and he glanced down, to see if Piper was watching him. She had her eyes closed, but it seemed to him that she was probably listening, so he continued. "—is supposed to be cooking eggs for supper. Alice and Lucas are getting the younger kids ready for bed. Alice knows where the diapers are."

"All right. Thank you for letting me know. Isn't Ingrid a little young to be cooking?"

"She's done it before." Gideon spoke for Piper who still had her eyes closed. "With Piper's supervision, of course. But I'm guessing Piper assumed you'd be able to watch her."

He hoped he wasn't saying anything out of turn, but he didn't want Ingrid to get in trouble for cooking, after the look that she had given Piper when her mom had asked her to do it.

"All right. I have Miss June and Miss Helen coming. Both of them need a little bit more time than me. So, between the three of us, we should be able to take care of six kids and supervise the cooking."

"You can call my buddies for reinforcements, or call me and I'll call them, if you need them." He glanced down at Piper. "That's all right with you?"

She nodded, the lines around her eyes tightening, her hands never loosening their hold on his neck, as he stepped around to the passenger side of his pickup, where Miss April had the door hanging wide open.

"I'm guessing this is probably going to hurt no matter how you do it, but I'll try to do my best to not bump it on anything," he murmured as he shifted her around the door, wishing he had picked her up the opposite way, because her feet were facing backward, and her head was pointed toward the windshield.

"I suppose this is one of those times where it would have been easier if we had put a little more thought into our position before we got here," Piper murmured, her eyes still squeezed tightly shut.

She had peeked to see where they were—he'd seen her—then closed them again, like the idea of trying to twist around was more than she could handle with her eyes open.

"I can put your butt on the seat, and once we have that settled, I'll keep my arms under your knees, and I'll spin you. Slowly."

"Thanks for adding the slowly. That made me feel a lot better about that suggestion."

He thought she was making a joke, and he grunted, gratified when her lips tilted up.

He was relieved that she wasn't taking this as seriously as he figured most people would. His buddies would be joking by now. Although, he would be joking a little more aggressively if it were one of them instead of Piper. Joking about tossing them in the pickup, rather than trying to figure out a way that would make them hurt the least.

Of course, he would never do such a thing, but he would definitely pick on them a lot more. With Piper...he felt a lot more protective. Not only did he not want to hurt her physically, but he wanted to protect her and let her know that he was protecting her. With his buddies, they would know it, and they would expect him to joke about it.

Piper was just...different.

Maybe that wasn't supposed to be such a revelation; after all, she was a woman. But he didn't typically feel like this about anyone, male or female.

He set her down on the seat and shifted his hand away from her back, making sure she wasn't going to fall out, before he put that arm under her legs and said, "Are you ready?"

"Yeah. Go ahead. If it hurts, it hurts. We need to get me in here somehow."

"True, but we want to do it in the least painful way possible."

"Thank you. I'm in agreement with that."

She seemed a little out of breath, and her hands, while they'd moved so that she had one hand on each of his shoulders, still gripped him tightly.

"On the count of three?"

"Just do it."

He grinned, turning her carefully, gently holding her hurt leg.

"You know, you two could have called an ambulance," Miss April said, startling Gideon, since he'd forgotten that she was still there.

"We could have." Gideon laughed because he hadn't even thought about it. Not like he would have if she'd been bleeding and he'd been concerned about saving her life.

"The kids would have loved it, but I would much prefer to ride in with less bells and whistles, so I'm glad we didn't." Piper's voice was soft, and her jaw jutted out, like she was determined not to give in to pain. But she was at least settled in the seat, and her eyes were open. "Thank you. I think you can shut the door."

"All right." He hesitated for a moment, then he said, "Would you like me to put your seat belt on first?"

She started to reach for it, then grimaced. "Would you mind?"

"Not at all. I kinda thought that maybe when you got settled, you wouldn't want to move except to breathe."

"If I could get away with not breathing, I think I would be happy with that too."

"That might present us with more difficulties," he said. She grunted in response. "Hopefully the pain will settle down again."

"It wasn't as bad as what I thought it was going to be."

"All right, here goes," he said, pulling her seat belt down, pulling it out, and giving it plenty of room to wrap around and click on the other side of her.

Her breath fanned against his neck, and she trembled slightly. He wanted to stop and put his arms around her, not to pick her up and carry her, but to hold her and comfort her.

Such an odd desire. Maybe it was because of the scent he'd picked up, sweet and a little sad at the same time. But it spoke strength and peace to him. It was light, and he could barely smell it, and he wanted to stay where he was and breathe deeply, trying to examine it and figure out exactly what it was.

Silly.

Erin would tell him to grow up.

There he was thinking about Erin again, when he hadn't thought of her in years.

"All right, I'm going to run over to my side, and then we'll head out. Any last-minute instructions for Miss April?" he asked as he stood back away from the pickup, his hand on the door, getting ready to close it.

"No. Just thank her. And thank you. I... I don't like this feeling of helplessness, and I really appreciate you stepping up without me having to ask."

He paused for just a moment. Not surprised, exactly, that she would thank him, but that she appreciated him taking charge. It wasn't necessarily something he was good at, but someone had needed to step in. He hadn't necessarily felt like he was doing a great job.

"I hope I haven't been acting out of turn," he said, his hand on the door, wanting to close it but lingering.

"You haven't. I am so glad you were here. I know I would have figured something out if you hadn't been, but you made it so much easier for me."

"God knew. He's the one who made it easier."

Her lips turned up, and she smiled, cracking her eyes and looking at him. Their gazes met, and he had that feeling again, that feeling that they were thinking along the same lines, that they understood each other, that they were experiencing the same things. He wasn't sure exactly what it was, but he had never felt it before, and he was a little taken aback that it would settle down and feel just right with Piper.

He nodded his head, just as much to break the spell as to get himself moving, before he stepped back and closed the door more carefully than he might normally, although surely closing the door didn't shake the pickup enough to make her foot hurt.

Just in case, he was careful.

"I'll keep you updated with what the docs say, although I suspect we'll be back late tonight. Maybe not with a cast, but with an appointment to get one."

"You guys just take your time. Don't rush back because of us. We know how to take care of kids, and they'll be in good hands until you get here."

"Thanks," he said, walking with Miss April to the middle of the pickup, where she turned right to go up the walk and he continued around.

She was going up the porch steps as he hopped in the truck and turned the engine over. This wasn't exactly how he had planned to spend his afternoon and evening, but he didn't feel put out. In fact, that last statement with Piper, where he told her that God had orchestrated it, felt exactly right to him.

God really *had* orchestrated it. And he felt like he was doing exactly what God wanted him to do. That was a good feeling.

Chapter 5

P iper sat in Gideon's pickup, morose.

The clock on his console read 12:37 AM.

He'd tried to engage her in conversation, but she had been hard-pressed to dredge up anything more than one-word answers. It wasn't just because she was tired, although she was completely exhausted, and the pain meds they'd given her were probably contributing to her desire to just lay her head back and go to sleep.

To give up.

She couldn't give up. She had her kids to consider, but the doctor had just told her she was to stay off her foot, sitting down with it propped up and preferably lying down with it higher than her head.

He had told her that she needed to have an appointment to get a cast, but with the blizzard that was coming, it might be next week, seven whole days, until she could see the specialist who would tell her whether she would be able to have it in a boot or not.

In the meantime, she was to stay off it. Completely off her feet.

She had spent the last of her money that she earned last week to pay the mortgage. She had counted on earning money the first three days of this week to buy groceries to weather the storm.

What was the saying? Man makes plans and God laughs? He had known that she planned to use those three days so she could feed her kids, and He'd also known that she wasn't going to be able to.

What was she going to do?

"I texted Miss April. She said Miss June and Miss Helen left after the kids went to bed. She'll be watching for us to come, then she's leaving."

Gideon's voice was low and serious from the other side of the truck.

"All right. Thank you." She wasn't sure what else she was supposed to say. Maybe it was because her brain was fuzzy, or maybe it's because she was feeling about as depressed as she had ever felt.

She had probably been lower after her husband had died, but she hadn't had this hopeless feeling. This feeling that she'd tried everything she could, given everything she could, put all the effort in that she could, and it just was not enough.

"I was going to stay. I... I know you didn't ask for it, but you're supposed to stay off your foot. How are you going to send your kids to school in the morning if you can't walk around to get them breakfast?"

"You don't have to do that." She gave in to the temptation to lay her head back on the seat and close her eyes. Her face tilted up toward the top of the pickup. "I can figure something out."

"I didn't think I had to," Gideon said slowly. "But I didn't want you there by yourself. I...feel partly responsible for the fact that you broke your foot. Let me help you."

She shook her head, tempted to smile, but too tired to make the effort. "It wasn't anyone's fault. I should make the kids pick up their toys more than I do. My mom would never let her house look that way."

"Kids need to have their toys out in order to play with them. No one puts their stuff away constantly without fail. Even adults. You can't expect perfection from children."

Her mom had. Her mom had expected perfection from her before she even went to kindergarten.

Thinking of her mom made her realize that she hadn't even told her that she was going to the ER. Maybe she should have. But her mom would probably insist on coming out, and then she would insist on cleaning everything, because nothing would have been cleaned to her specifications, and Piper would have to listen to how she was a terrible housekeeper, and how she wasn't a good mother, and how her kids were getting away with things that she should discipline them for, and if she admitted to her mom that she didn't have enough money to buy groceries, her mom would get on her about the fact that she'd told her she should go to college, and if she had gone to college, her life would have magically worked out.

She didn't want to listen to it.

She might not have a choice.

It might be something she had to do in order to get her kids to eat.

Or the man beside her was offering to stay. He wouldn't buy her groceries, she couldn't let him even if he did offer, but he would help.

"I don't want to impose, but I do want to help. If it bothers you, let me stay just until the kids get to school. Although, you still have, what? Three kids left at home?"

"Yeah. And... I'm going to have to cancel my appointments for today. Although, I think maybe I'll try and see if I can at least get a few in."

"No. The doctor told you to stay off your feet. You will have to cancel them all. You can't cut hair sitting down."

"But I have people who are depending on me."

"This is not a life-or-death situation. They are depending on you to get a haircut. Not have heart surgery. You can cancel your appointments."

There was an edge to his last sentence that surprised her. Like he really cared about whether or not she was standing on her foot when she wasn't supposed to be.

"I need the money."

There.

There was no point in beating around the bush, arguing with him trying to convince him that she thought it was okay to go against the doctor's orders. She didn't. She would do what he told her to do, except she couldn't. She had to earn money so she could feed her children. She hadn't known this was going to happen, of course, or she wouldn't have sent that mortgage payment. It would be better for the mortgage to be late than for her kids not to eat.

"You can't need the money so badly that you would risk your foot healing incorrectly and you not being able to work for the rest of your life."

He had a point. If her foot didn't heal properly, the doctor said that standing on it would be painful for the rest of her life. That scared her. Her job required her to be on her feet. She had no choice about it. She didn't want to be addicted to popping pain pills for the rest of her life just to be able to work.

But if that's what it took, that's what she would have to do. She'd always made whatever sacrifice was necessary in order for her to raise her children and do the best for them.

But she didn't argue with Gideon. He wouldn't understand. Someone like him, a single man who had no dependents, no one depending on him for everything, he was free, with no ties. He could go wherever he wanted to go and do whatever he wanted to, and the only one affected would be him.

It had been so long since she had that kind of freedom. She couldn't remember what it was like. Actually, she'd gone from her mother's overbearing and overcontrolling home to being married to her husband.

Her husband had been a good man. Richard had loved her and wanted her to succeed in whatever she tried to do, but still, when a person was married, it was no longer just about them but about their spouse first.

At least that's the way she looked at it.

So, technically, she'd never had the kind of freedom where she could just go wherever she wanted and do whatever she wanted.

While that sounded good, she wouldn't want to give up her children in order to gain that kind of freedom. She couldn't imagine life without them. Of course, there was a time when she couldn't imagine life without Richard either.

"I have a feeling that you're not agreeing with me. But maybe it's the drugs."

"You're just jealous because they wouldn't give you any." She kept her eyes closed and her head back, thankful to have a lighter topic to talk about, rather than her financial situation.

"That's true. I am a little jealous. You better keep your hands tight on your purse, because I'm liable to dip into them, if you keep giving me this kind of grief."

"I'm not giving you any grief. I'm setting you free."

"I'm not a butterfly you're holding in your hand."

He said that with so much derision in his voice, she laughed.

"I did not mistake you for a butterfly. I promise."

"All right. I'm glad we have that settled. Now, if I could just get you to agree with me on some of these other things I wanted to talk to you about."

"I'm not disagreeing. I just know that you have other things you need to do. You don't need to stay at my house and help me with my kids. I... I can do it." She wasn't entirely sure that she could do it. It was all she could do to control the chaos when she had two good feet and could stand in the middle of it. She was fairly certain she was not going to be controlling anything flat on her back on the couch.

But she couldn't take advantage of Gideon's generosity any longer. After all, while she hadn't just met him that day, she had talked to him, had a real conversation with him, for the first time, and then he ended up taking her to the ER. He didn't need to spend more time with her.

"Is there a reason you don't like me?" he asked after they'd driven a few more miles in silence.

They were about halfway home, and she wasn't sure whether she'd be able to stay awake for the rest of the trip. She appreciated him talking to her. Not only did she like the rumble of his voice—it made something in her chest feel deliciously good—but she appreciated the idea that there was someone beside her, even if it was only temporary.

"What made you think I don't like you?" she asked, slitting her eyes and looking over at him.

He glanced at her, his eyes running over her face as though making sure that she was okay, before he looked back at the road, his hands gripping the top of the steering wheel.

"I offer to help you, and you call me a butterfly. It's a little hard on a man's ego when a lady does that to him. Turns him down, calls him an insect, and insults his manhood."

"So you feel rejected? And misunderstood?" She was mostly teasing, answering him the way she would if one of her children were complaining about not being treated right.

"Yes. That's exactly how I feel. And the only way you can fix it is by letting me help you."

"All right. I can't imagine why you would want to, but I think I'm too tired, or the drugs are too strong, and no, you can't have any, to argue."

"And that's another reason I know you don't like me. You won't share your drugs."

"That's illegal. For all I know, you could be an undercover FBI agent, just tempting me to step one toe over the line, and then where would I be?"

"In prison," he supplied easily.

She huffed out a laugh. "Exactly, and what would become of my children?"

"I guess then you'd accept my help, now wouldn't you?"

"My mom would probably come and take over my house, and she'd put up with you exactly three seconds before she kicked you out. Nothing to do with you, and everything to do with her."

"She sounds like a nice lady," Gideon said, grinning at her.

She put her head back on the seat again, pointing it at the ceiling, and smiled. "She's a good lady in her own way. But she is best taken in small doses. Very small doses."

"Does she know you broke your foot in two different places?"

"She does not. When I tell her that, I'll have to tell her that I stepped on a toy tractor, and then I'll have to listen to her tell me how I need to do a better job teaching my children to put their toys away, and I guess it's the drugs, sorry to keep bringing them up, but I just don't feel up to that."

"You do keep inserting that little dig about how you have all the good drugs into our conversation. I'd like for you to do a background check on me, so I can prove I'm not FBI, so we can share without guilt."

"I'll tell you what, I'll give you the drugs, if you go home and don't give me any more grief about standing on my foot."

"No deal."

"But I thought you really wanted the drugs?" she asked, not really teasing, because she kind of figured that he'd take that, if not in reality, because she didn't have any illusions about the fact that he would never take her pain pills, but hypothetically he would accept.

"Not as much as I want to see you heal up the way you're supposed to. And I told you, I feel responsible."

She didn't want to be his responsibility. That he was there because of guilt, although he couldn't be there for anything else, because it wasn't exactly like they were friends. Although, she would really like to have someone like him as her friend. Someone who was funny, made her laugh, teased her out of her seriousness, and encouraged her to do things that she normally wouldn't.

Richard had been very much like that. Although, he hadn't been as masculine as Gideon was. There was just a confidence about Gideon that, along with the smile that constantly lurked around his mouth and made his eyes twinkle, drew her out of her serious nature.

She didn't want to change his smile, she wanted to be drawn into it.

But for one, she figured he was younger than she was, and for another, no man in his right mind would want to have anything to do with a woman and her six kids.

Even as a friend.

There was too much drama in her life. Too much constant upheaval.

So, guilt drove him, and she didn't want it to.

But he wasn't taking no for an answer very well, and she was tired.

"All right. You feel responsible. So, stay tonight, help get the kids ready for school in the morning, and then do whatever it was you were going to do tomorrow." Or today rather. She looked at the clock again, realizing that tomorrow was indeed today, and she hadn't made it to bed yet. Morning would be here before she knew it, and while she loved the fact that the pills had taken most of the pain away, she didn't want to be groggy in the morning. She had a lot of work to do.

"I was going to spend the day with you, working on your addition," he clarified.

Oh, that was right. Well, he was just going to have to accept the fact that she wasn't going to be able to follow the doctor's orders. But no point in arguing about that anymore this evening, um, morning.

"All right then. I guess it works out pretty well anyway."

"I guess it does." He pulled into her drive, slowly moving to the house.

"Is that the steer that runs around Sweet Water?" he asked as he pulled the truck to a stop and cut the motor.

"Yeah. I don't know why he's been hanging around my house lately, but he has. He actually seemed to bring squirt guns, which is weird, but they showed up at the same time he did. We've been all over the property, and I never saw them anywhere before. But the first day we saw him, he was out there standing over the top of four squirt guns. The kids have been having a blast with them, even though it's really not warm enough for water games."

"When you live in North Dakota, your capacity for water games starts at a much lower temperature than normal people."

She laughed, because it was true. Kids loved water. It didn't matter what state they lived in, they wanted to play in it year-round. Even if it froze while they were doing so.

Chapter 6

"Now, I don't want you to take this the wrong way, but I'm going to walk around the pickup, and I'm going to carry you into the house."

"I think I'll let you. The pain has finally subsided, and I'm a little afraid that if I move, it's going to come back. I think I'll sleep a lot better if my foot isn't throbbing all night."

"I'm sure you'll sleep better. And that was a lot easier than I thought it was going to be. You seem to argue with me about everything. I was just bracing myself for it."

"I think you have it backward. You're the one that argues with me over everything, and I'm just trying to win one small argument with you. Just one. That's all I ask."

"All right. I'll let you win the next argument we have. As long as it's about something that I don't care about."

Piper laughed as Gideon got out. Appreciating the fact that even at one o'clock in the morning, he wasn't grumpy or touchy, but was still joking with her and making her smile.

He would make a great father.

The thought came unbidden into her head as he was walking around the truck.

It was true, he would. Patience was a major requisite, as well as the ability to roll with things. Gideon seemed to have both of those abilities.

Even better than she did. She'd had to work on hers. With each child, she had to pray and ask God to help her be better. Mostly with rolling with things. The patience wasn't as hard. Not for her, since she'd had a tendency to make childish mistakes when she was a kid, and she knew how helpless and hopeless she felt when her mom expected her to be perfect.

Giving grace for imperfections was a lot easier than having patience when she had six kids crying and complaining and fighting and whining.

Those were the times where she'd like to be able to go into the bathroom and close the door, but she always had a child that was small enough that she figured they'd pick up some kind of little thing from the floor and choke on it while she was having a meltdown in the bathroom. So she'd never given herself that luxury.

The truck door opened, and she shook herself out of her contemplations.

"All right, gonna try to do this without jiggling you again. I've had a little practice today, and I think I might be getting better at it."

She laughed, because they'd had a whole discussion about which way she should be facing when he carried her around to the truck from the hospital.

The ER nurse had looked at them like they were crazy, and then just smiled and shook her head when he went from one side of her bed to the other then back to the first side as they figured out which direction his truck was parked and which direction she'd need to be facing.

Piper had explained to the nurse the problem they'd had when he'd set her in the first time, and the nurse had laughed.

She said they made a cute couple as they were walking out of the exam room.

Piper didn't think Gideon had heard it, and she pretended not to hear either. That was enough to make her feel awkward, but since

Gideon didn't have any reaction at all, it made it easier for her to shove the thought aside as well.

"I'm glad I can get you practiced up. You never know when you're going to have to do it for real," she said.

"Yeah. This is just practice. So if I bump your foot, it really doesn't matter. It's not going to keep you from sleeping a wink tonight because of the sharp pain you have to deal with or anything."

"Exactly. I wouldn't want you to have that kind of pressure when you've never done this before," she said, rather fatalistically, with drama in her voice as well. She supposed it was immature of them to pretend that they were doing what they were actually doing, but both of them seemed to be entertained by it, and she kind of thought it was funny that they seemed to have the same sense of humor, one that was just a little bit on the immature side.

Richard always got a little annoyed with her when she got too goofy. He liked to make people smile, but he didn't like goofiness.

She crossed the line too much for him sometimes.

She had a feeling that she and Gideon would play off each other, and he would really bring her goofy side out. Which scared her a little, because she was a mother of six and she needed to be serious and responsible.

Miss April met them at the door as Gideon carefully carried her up the steps. She held it while he walked in, quietly said that the kids had gone to bed without any problems, and then said good night and walked to her car.

Piper hadn't expected her to stay, it was late after all, and she was probably usually in bed well before this.

"Did you want me to take you to your bedroom? Or do you want me to put you on the couch?"

"The couch is where I sleep," she said, feeling the events of the day weighing down on her and the responsibilities of tomorrow pulling like an anchor around her neck.

"I think I heard that from somewhere. Maybe from you, although it seems like a long time ago."

"I know. This day has felt like three days all shoved together."

"I bet it has. When you're in pain, time seems to drag."

"I'm not going to argue with that. It sucks your energy like water down the drain."

"Where are your blankets?" he asked as he set her carefully on the couch.

"Don't yell at me, but they're behind the couch along with my pillows. That's how I make my bed in the morning. I just throw everything behind the couch."

She was way too tired to try to hide the fact that she was a terrible housekeeper. Her mother would absolutely die if she knew that she didn't even bother to fold stuff but just tossed it between the couch and the wall until that evening when she needed it.

"Clever. I like it. I could get rid of my bed, because it would be a lot easier to make it if I did that."

"If your mother would have as much a problem with it as mine does, might not be worth it," she said. "I just do it because I have to."

He helped her arrange her pillows, carefully placing one under her broken foot while she grimaced.

When he spoke, it was on a completely different subject. "I'm sorry that it took me so long to get out here to start on your addition. But I was very sympathetic to your break and pain today, since that's what kept me home."

"That's right. I'd actually forgotten about that."

She was surprised they hadn't talked about it while they were sitting in the waiting room of the ER. Although that was one of the nice things about a small-town hospital, there hadn't been too many other patients in, just someone who was inebriated and had run into a lamppost, thinking he was picking up a woman from the things he was muttering, and split his skull open, needing a few stitches. His buddies, who were just as sloshed as he was, had made a lot of noise, but the group was basically harmless. More of an annoyance than anything. Since the doctor couldn't say anything without them laughing.

She kind of felt that the physician on duty was happy to see people who hadn't been drinking, although Piper didn't feel any more intelligent than anyone else considering that she'd fallen and broken her foot in her own house. At least they'd been out on the town.

"I didn't want to minimize your pain by talking about mine. But it definitely brought back memories. Only I fell on ice."

"North Dakota has a lot of that in the winter," she said, feeling her blanket settle around her. She hadn't expected him to cover her up with it. Just hand it to her.

"I take it these pillows you want under your head?" he asked, pulling more out from behind the couch.

"If you just set them there, I can take care of them. I need a moment."

His hand slid behind her head, lifting it up.

She smiled.

"I thought I was going to win the next argument?" she reminded him gently.

"I didn't argue with you."

"You didn't let me win."

"I decided that no one learns anything if you are just allowed to win. You have to earn your win. That way you appreciate it, and you get stronger and better."

"All right. You're going to try to make the poor wounded woman, who can't even walk, stronger and better. Thanks."

"Tough love here," he said, slipping the pillow underneath her raised head and then adjusting it. "How's that?"

"It doesn't feel like tough love."

"There's one more pillow, and I kind of feel like it should go under your foot. The doctor said to keep it elevated."

"That's fine with me," she said wearily, knowing that tomorrow she would have to be on it, so she should probably follow his instructions to the letter while she could.

"I'm not sure that I'm going to be able to lift it higher without hurting you; I wanted to warn you."

"We want to follow the doctor's directions, so I will grit my teeth and bear it," she said, giving an exaggerated grimace, to show how brave she was being.

"Well. If only you had been that brave all evening."

"Are you serious? I did not cry one time, not once. I think I should get some credit for that."

"Yeah. I probably should give you credit, considering I cried at least four different times the night I broke my leg."

"Really?" she asked, her eyes flying open.

"No. But it sounded good, didn't it?"

"You lied!" she exclaimed, with false outrage.

"No. I was just teasing you. You realized it was a lie right away."

"No. I believed you."

"Really?"

"Hmm. I'm not sure our friendship is strong enough for me to be able to answer that honestly right now. If you're still talking to me when you're finished with the addition, you can ask me again, and I'll give you my honest answer."

"Our friendship is strong enough for you to be honest with me." The teasing was gone from his eyes, and he looked down at her, his expression completely serious.

The humor faded from her face, and she got the feeling that he had heard her say she couldn't afford not to work, and while she thought that she had successfully changed the subject and distracted him from her problems, she thought now that maybe he just shoved it aside to talk about later, and later had come.

46

"What's the money situation?" he asked and somehow managed to sound compassionate and stern at the same time.

"I just spent everything I had in the checkbook to pay the mortgage. I was hoping to work the next three days so I could buy groceries for us so we could weather the storm. That's the situation."

She appreciated the blankets and the snuggly warm feeling she felt, and the fact that her foot only throbbed a little, and that she felt cozy and safe on the couch. She closed her eyes and said, "Now you know why I don't have any choice but to keep the clients and schedule that I have tomorrow. But I'll keep my foot elevated tonight. I promise."

"I know no such thing. What I do know is that after I get the kids up, feed them breakfast, and get them off to school, the three little ones and I are going to go get groceries. If you have a preference as to what you want your kids to eat, make out a list. Otherwise, I'm really good at making boxed mac and cheese and hot dogs, and sometimes I even throw a can of peas in with it, if I'm feeling like I need to be healthy."

"Wow. I really want to think that you're kidding, but I have a really bad feeling that...you're not."

"No. I'm dead serious about that. Although, once, about ten years ago, I did eat a carrot. It was an accident, but still, it happened."

"Wow. All right. I'll make a list." She was laughing despite herself and thinking that maybe she had just agreed to allow him to buy her groceries, when she was supposed to be fighting with him, but he'd made it so funny and she agreed before she realized what she was doing. Which was probably his intention all along, although he didn't seem like the kind of man who angled to get his way. He just joked his way into getting his way.

She closed her eyes and shook her head.

"That's better. I like a woman who knows her place."

She laughed. "Shut up. There are so many things wrong with that I don't even know where to start."

"The drugs are my friend. They get her to go to sleep and quit arguing, and at that point, she's rather easy to get along with."

"Yes. Yes, I am. I am the easiest person you've ever had the privilege of carrying around and getting along with."

Chapter 7

G ideon moved to the wall and turned out the lights.

He had been going to ask Piper if there were any extra blankets or pillows anywhere, but she seemed so tired, and she'd been such a trooper all evening. She hadn't complained, even though he could tell how bad it hurt. Having just gone through a bad break himself, the pain was still fresh in his mind.

A couple of times, he'd wanted to grab a hold of the doctor, who seemed to be rougher than necessary, but maybe that was just his imagination, because he already felt bad enough that Piper had been going through so much.

The doctor had been good at his job and had been professionally compassionate.

Gideon's emotions had definitely crossed the line from professional. He wasn't sure exactly what that meant, other than he found Piper to be fun and funny despite the fact that not only did she have a broken foot and was dealing with that pain, but she was also dealing with the fact that she needed to work in order to buy groceries for her family.

He hadn't wanted her to know how shocked he was that she was living that close to the edge.

He thought he'd done a good job covering with humor, which was his personality.

Pulling his phone out of his pocket, he opened the back door as quietly as he could and slipped outside.

It was a beautiful North Dakota night, with thousands of stars in the sky and a quarter moon sitting low-slung above the horizon, lying there, looking up. Maybe admiring the stars too.

Gideon grinned a little at the image, but his heart wasn't as light as it usually was. He...wanted... No. He needed to help Piper. He couldn't do anything less.

Dialing Baker's number, he waited impatiently with the phone pressed to his ear for Baker to answer.

"You'd better not be calling because you need my help changing a tire. We've already been through that once after midnight, and never again."

"You're always chipper when I wake you up in the middle of the night. Do you need a minute?"

Gideon grinned, knowing that Baker was covering his concern with grumpiness.

They all had their things, he supposed. Although he'd much rather someone cover their feelings with humor than anger.

Baker wasn't an angry person. He just had a tendency to be brusque when he was worried.

"I don't need a minute. I'm not a snowflake. Tell me you're not dead."

"If I were dead, I would be haunting you, not calling you."

"Did you need something? Or are you just calling to annoy me?"

"Mostly calling to annoy you, but I also want my phone charger and a couple changes of clothes, and if you can do it without swishing it in the toilet, I want my toothbrush, too. But if you can't keep yourself from acting like a freckle-face, junior high, snot-nose kid, just forget about the toothbrush. I'll do without."

"That's disgusting. I would never do that to your toothbrush."

"I didn't want you thinking you needed to get me back for the time I did it to yours. So, just throwing that out there."

"Wait. What? You put my toothbrush in the toilet on purpose?"

"Didn't I ever tell you about that?" Gideon grinned. He knew Baker wouldn't really believe him but would still be running the last time Gideon had touched his toothbrush through his head, which was the previous summer when they'd gone to a farming convention.

Gideon had taken his toothbrush out of the package, and before he had given it to Baker, he'd run it under the cold water tap. He then told Baker that he twisted it around in the toilet.

He really had Baker going before he told him he was kidding. Now, he had him going again.

"You told me you were kidding."

"I know. But I was kidding about kidding. You know?"

"No. I don't know. That's disgusting."

"I think you've already said that. You need to expand your vocabulary."

"I have some four-letter words that would help me expand my vocabulary and vent a little of the frustration that I'm feeling with my friend right now. Using the word friend very, very loosely."

"Calm down. Are you awake yet?"

"I'm wide awake. Thank you."

"Hey. No problem. I am at Piper's house. She is the woman I was supposed to be working for today."

"You'd better not hurt her."

"You don't even know her."

"I don't need to know her in order to know that I'll come wring your neck if you did something to her."

"What makes you think I did something to her?"

"It's one o'clock in the morning. I also heard a rumor about her falling."

"Well, actually, it was partially my fault that she fell. And broke her foot."

"I knew it! I knew you had done something to her. Man, you are like a walking disaster. Especially when it comes to women."

"That is not the slightest bit true. First of all, I am not—"

"Anyway. Forget it. Did I mention it is one o'clock in the morning? Spit out what you want to say, and let me get back to bed. Some of us have to work tomorrow."

"I'm working too. Calm yourself."

"You have five seconds to tell me before I hang up on you."

"You really need to learn to wake up happy."

"He's in the other room."

Gideon grunted. "She really did break her foot. I need my stuff. Whatever you grab will be fine. Just a couple changes of clothes, I'll do my wash here if I need to, and my charger. I'll need that. If I'm not here, just set the stuff on the porch."

"If you're going to be there, why can't you come out and get it?"

"I need to get groceries, and I'm going to have three kids with me. I've never done that before, but I'm guessing that we probably ought to get the groceries really fast, while they're in a good mood, and I'm not going to want to take the time to do anything else."

"All right. Forget I asked. You want your charger, and you want a couple of old dresses. Got it."

"Right, dresses. Good luck finding those."

"I can find some pink dresses pretty easily. And after what you did with my toothbrush, I think I'm justified. It will give me a little satisfaction. Better than the four-letter words I was gonna say."

"You really need to take some anger management classes. This whole needing to get people back whenever they joke with you is just ridiculous."

"All right. Toothbrush and forget the dresses. You want bedsheets instead, and if you keep arguing with me, I'll cut the bedsheets into ribbons and deliver those."

"Hey. Don't mess with my bedsheets, those are the nicest bedsheets I've ever had."

"You are the only person I know who really gives a flip about the sheets you lie on."

"That's because I have culture and class. Something that you need to work on. And I'm going to keep calling and getting you up in the middle of the night until you answer without being a grouch."

"Glad you didn't wreck." There was a pause. "You didn't wreck, right?"

"No. She stepped on a toy tractor and fell. And there were no other injuries other than her broken foot."

"All right. Take care."

"Go back to sleep. Think about toilets and toothbrushes."

He slid his phone off. Smiling.

That was the nice thing about being friends with people for such a long time that he could mess with them and totally know they got him.

He leaned against the porch post, staring up at the stars. Thinking about the evening. How much fun it had been with Piper.

If she didn't have six children, he'd be asking her out. For sure.

They clicked in a way that he had with very few people.

Not even that they had so much in common, just that he felt at ease with her. She got his humor, and he admired her. A lot.

Lord, why couldn't You send me a woman just like that?

A lot of silence met that question. Like he'd figured. God hadn't been in a big hurry to send him anyone, after the mess he'd made with Erin.

It was almost like the Lord was saying *I tried, and you didn't cooperate, so I gave up on you.*

He didn't really believe that, but the Lord definitely was taking His good old time.

But now that he met Piper, he knew exactly the kind of woman he wanted. Someone who was serious but not afraid to laugh. Who took her responsibility seriously but didn't get overly upset when things spiraled out of control. Who had plenty of grace to give to cover his mistakes.

Why would I need to send you a woman like Piper, when you have Piper herself?

He blinked. It wasn't an audible voice, but the thought was clear in his head.

Lord? She has six kids!

He wasn't sure whether it was God's voice or the devil. It felt a lot like a temptation he would have to resist. After all, no man would be crazy enough to...fall? Was that the right word? Was he falling for Piper?

After one evening together, it was way too soon to tell.

Wasn't it?

He supposed it wasn't too soon to tell someone had character and integrity and the kind of character that he wanted in his life. But six kids?

He was totally fine with helping her. He felt like he owed her. After all, she might have fallen, but she was looking back to talk to him, and that was all his fault.

Plus, he couldn't leave her without recourse.

He would go tomorrow, buy her groceries, and then he could talk to Miss April, see if the town could do something for her. Have some kind of benefit or something. He didn't know what, but they'd come up with something, and by the time he was done with the addition, they would be taking care of her, he would feel better about everything, and he would be free to move on.

Through it all, he might have made a friend. Because, despite the six kids, he really did like Piper. And he definitely would like to have someone like that as a friend.

Just as a friend.

Chapter 8

"I don't want jelly on my sandwich,"

"I don't want peanut butter on mine."

"I want mine cut across. It makes it taste better."

Gideon stood in the middle of the kitchen, knife in hand, the peanut butter and jelly open in front of him, and feeling as confused as he'd ever felt in his life before.

"One at a time. Or I might not get them right," he said, laughing, because even if they did it one at a time, he still might not get it right.

"They will eat them however you make them. And they'll be grateful that there's someone making their sandwiches for them." Piper's voice came from the couch in the living room.

Far from helping Gideon, he felt like it put him even further into the corner. Now who was he going to listen to?

"I'll eat mine with jelly on it, but I hate jelly. Mom doesn't make me eat it," Lucas said, and Gideon nodded.

"How about this. I think I need one sandwich with just peanut butter, one sandwich with just jelly, and one sandwich cut diagonally. I'll do that, and then each of you make sure you pick up the correct sandwich, okay?"

The three heads nodded as he stood on the other side of the island countertop and started making the sandwiches.

"There should be one stalk of celery left in the refrigerator, and you can put cream cheese on that for your lunch as well."

"All right. You guys get the stalk of celery, and I'll cut it into three pieces."

"I'll get the cream cheese," Alice said, turning back to the refrigerator and pulling out both the celery and cream cheese.

He'd never heard of celery and cream cheese, but the kids weren't complaining about that, so he wouldn't either.

"Do we have any Chex mix left?" Lucas asked, calling into the room where his mom lay on the couch, Luna standing beside her head, stroking her hair, and probably not knowing what to do because she wasn't used to seeing her mom lie on the couch.

Theodora hadn't gotten up yet, although he thought he might have heard her in the room. He wasn't sure how anyone could sleep through all the noise that had been happening in the house since about six o'clock this morning, but it was 6:45, and Theodora had seemed to manage it for at least forty-five minutes anyway.

"No, it's all gone," Piper called. "But I think there are three brownies left. You can take those. And there are three apples as well."

None of the kids looked overly excited about the apples, but Gideon dutifully put them in their bags, along with the brownies and celery, and then he gave each one their bag so they could drop the correct sandwich in.

"The bus will be here in five minutes. You guys need to get your coats and shoes on."

The kids grabbed their lunch bags and ran to the door, scrambling for their shoes, with Ingrid exclaiming, "Where's my paper? I set my paper right here, and it's gone!"

Gideon had barely had that warning before she burst into tears.

He remembered yesterday how Piper had taken a little extra time to talk to Ingrid, and he thought that maybe it was because she seemed to get lost in the crowd of kids.

He set the container of peanut butter down and walked over.

"Was it a white piece of paper?"

"Yes?" She looked up, her eyes red, tears leaking out of the corners.

"All right. I haven't seen it, but I'll know to look for a big white piece of paper. Are you sure you set it here?" he asked, his eyes skimming around the coats and boots and gloves and hats that sat by the door.

"I think so," Ingrid said, scrunching up her nose.

"Could it be in your room?"

"I don't think so, but I'll go look."

"I'll come with you. I hear Theodora anyway."

"She might be wet. She'll probably need a diaper change," Piper said, her tone holding a warning.

"Got it. I'll need a change of clothes after I deal with Theodora."

He heard her laughter as he turned and followed Ingrid into her room.

The baby stood in her crib, bouncing up and down, her eyes clouding over for just a moment as they landed on Gideon, but then she smiled when she saw Ingrid.

"Here it is!" Ingrid said, pulling a white piece of paper off the top of her dresser. "Maybe I didn't put it by the door after all."

"Maybe you did and then decided to move it so that you would be sure to see it on your dresser in the morning."

"Maybe," she said, running toward the door. "Thank you!" she shouted over her shoulder as she ran out of the bedroom.

It had been nothing but chaos since the first kid had woken up.

He wasn't quite used to getting up and hitting the floor running, taking care of minor emergency after minor emergency, but he couldn't say that it had been terrible. It definitely would be fun and not boring every day. Although, he could see how the fighting and bickering would grate on a person's nerves.

Still, it had been a happy kind of chaos, even the fighting. He felt like he was in the middle of a bunch of people who supported each other, and it was a good feeling.

"Do you remember me from yesterday?" he asked Theodora after flipping on the lights.

She didn't look like she remembered him. She looked like she was about ready to cry.

"I'll tell you what. I'll find a diaper and a change of clothes, and we'll go out and see Mom. I'll not change you until we get to her. Is that a deal?"

"Mama? Mama?"

"Yeah. Go see Mama."

Theodora didn't look like she was totally sold on the idea that she was going to see her actual mom, but he found the diapers, and Henry, the four-year-old, came in and showed him where the clean clothes were.

He appreciated Henry's help and felt a little bad for him, stuck in between all the girls, with two older sisters and two little sisters.

Maybe he should be happy for him, because if anything, Henry should be in touch with his feminine side.

Picking the baby up out of the crib, he set her on his hip and hauled her out of the room.

"Look what I found in there," he said as he set the baby down on the floor in front of Piper on the couch.

"Good morning, Theo," she said, chatting with the baby who smiled at seeing her mom and reached for her.

Piper put an arm around her. "I can change it."

"I got it. I've never done it before, so I brought her out because I might need instructions. Although, how hard can it be?"

"If she stays still, it shouldn't be too bad. If she doesn't, I'm not even sure I can get her diaper changed."

"All right. Your job is to make her stay still. My job is to figure out the diaper."

She showed him how to open it up and lay it on the ground, and then somehow he was supposed to get the baby on top of that after getting her wet diaper off her.

He figured there should be an easier way to do that, and maybe he'd start working on that at some point.

But for the time being, he just focused on taking the wet one off and putting the dry one on. It only took about ten minutes, and when it was finished, he felt like he had accomplished something for the day.

"Is there something in particular I should feed these guys?" he asked, since Luna, the two-year-old, had missed breakfast as well. Henry seemed like the kind of kid who probably would eat two breakfasts.

"If you don't mind, there's a bag of oatmeal in the cupboard. I like to try to make sure Luna gets some in the morning. It keeps her regular."

He thought Piper might be talking about bowel movements, but he didn't question her.

"A bag of oatmeal in the cupboard. Got it."

"And you could put Theodora in her high chair. She'll eat oatmeal too. But you have to spoon-feed her, or she'll get it everywhere."

"Okay. I can handle that."

He kept Theodora on his hip while he opened the cupboard.

"Not that one, two doors down."

He closed the cupboard door and opened the one two doors down.

He had been expecting a packet of oatmeal. She had said bag, but he had thought she didn't really mean it.

But when he opened the cupboard door, he saw the biggest bag of oatmeal he'd ever seen in his life. He knew it was oatmeal, because it was clear plastic and he could see the oatmeal in the bag. Not to mention, the sticker on the back said steel cut oats.

Could this be what she was talking about?

"When you said bag of oatmeal, you meant a literal bag of actual steel cut oats?" he asked, unsure how else to phrase the question other than coming right out and asking.

"Yes. I take it you've never used actual steel cut oats to make oatmeal?"

"Didn't know that was a thing. But how hard can it be?"

"It's not hard at all. You need to bring water to a boil and then add the oatmeal, and you simmer it for just a little bit, stirring. Then it will get thick. While you're waiting for that, you'll need to defrost the applesauce."

"You don't have it in a jar?" he asked, since that was the only way he'd ever eaten applesauce before.

"No. I have bags of applesauce in the freezer from when I canned it last fall. I...forgot to get any out yesterday. It was a little bit crazy last night."

"Yeah. Someone broke her foot and insisted that she be taken to the ER, and it just messed everything up."

"And then someone refused to leave, so now he's getting a real education about things like diapers and oatmeal and squabbling children." She laughed, and the sound made him smile. "I'm betting that you're not going to be begging me to stay again anytime soon."

"I actually was planning on staying tonight and tomorrow night. I figured I might as well do that, since I'll be working on the addition, and I'll help with the kids, too."

"We're supposed to get a blizzard in a few days."

"Is it going to be a hardship if you're snowed in with me?" he asked, pulling the bag of oatmeal down from the cupboard with the hand that wasn't holding Theodora.

He was actually surprised that Theodora didn't want down, but she seemed content riding around on his hip. Maybe she could see better from that position.

"It's not going to be a hardship for me, but if you can imagine this morning, and the chaos that you were standing in the middle of, only it lasts all day long. That's what it's like when the kids are home from school. And that's what it's like when it's snowing and they can't go outside."

"It wasn't too bad. I was actually thinking it was kind of fun. I mean, the fighting would get old, but it's fun to be in the middle of a big family, with activity going on all the time. I think it will get even better as they get older."

"You know, they do get fun as they get older. They're fun at age two, but Lucas and Alice have such personalities, and Ingrid has really come into her own in the last year or so."

"She's a sweetie. They all are," he said as he finished unwrapping the twisty tie around the end of the oatmeal and looked around for a measuring cup. "How much water, and how much oatmeal?"

She gave him the specs, and he measured everything out.

"Did you get your grocery list ready?"

"Yeah. I worked on it this morning when I woke up."

"You were up before the kids?" he asked, vaguely remembering that she'd been on her phone when he heard the first sound from the bedrooms. He hadn't asked her what she was doing.

"Yeah. Doesn't seem to matter what time I go to bed, I'm always up between four and five. I got the list made, but hadn't texted it to you, yet."

He set the water on the stove and turned the burner on as she pulled her phone out and sent him the list.

He had done some cooking, since he and his friends took turns doing the honors on the ranch they owned together. But he really did mostly cook mac and cheese and hot dogs. None of them were picky, and most of the time, they were working and just happy to have food on the table. No one got touchy about exactly what kind of food it was.

"I'm not expecting you to take the children with you when you do this, but I do really appreciate you getting the groceries. I promise I'll pay you back."

His phone buzzed with the text as she spoke, and he looked down to confirm it was from her before he looked into the room.

"I don't want payback. I'm taking the kids. All three of them. And that's all I want to talk about it."

She raised her brows at his high-handed tone and then grinned. He smiled back at her, and they shared a little humor, even though he hadn't really meant it that way, but he liked that she didn't take his bossiness as a challenge, or get offended over it, but just smiled.

He figured that he'd be hearing about it, if not this year, years from now, when she finally gave him the money back, they'd remember this moment and how she said she was going to do it.

Maybe that wasn't the way it was going to work out, but that's the way it felt.

He followed her instructions to get the applesauce out of the freezer and defrosted, and then finished making the oatmeal.

He had no idea how she did all of this work all day plus worked as a full-time beautician, making enough money to keep her small family afloat. He definitely had a lot more respect for how difficult it was.

All winter, when he'd been laid up with his own broken leg, Piper had been a mostly faceless woman with no personality.

Now that he'd spent a day with her, it was obvious she was anything but.

Of course, he couldn't have shown up any faster than he did with his broken leg, but he was glad that someone else hadn't taken over, and he'd gotten this opportunity.

Piper was certainly not what he expected.

Chapter 9

June adjusted the scarf on her head. Not because it was cold outside, but because it was so warm. Her scalp was itchy. But she wasn't complaining, since her hair was growing back in. Little sprigs of peach fuzz dotting her head.

Cancer had been quite a journey, but her treatments had ended, and her last appointment had been as good as she could expect it to be.

She needed to wait a few more months before she was given the total all clear, but for now, she was gaining strength, the effects of the chemo dissipating with each day, as her energy came back.

She felt well enough to go visit her old friend Terry.

Clicking the key fob to lock her car, she stepped onto the sidewalk in Rockerton, walking down two houses to Terry's place.

Twenty years ago, when they were raising their children together, Terry's husband had worked with June's. Their families had done a lot together, and then Wayne had gotten fired.

He had told her it was because the people who had worked there for years were jealous of him coming in and shaking things up. He worked so hard that he made them look bad, and they got angry at him.

It made sense to June, because while Wayne had never been overly kind to her, he was a hard worker. She could definitely give him that.

Regardless, after that, she and Terry had drifted apart.

But recently, Terry had been diagnosed with cancer, and June, because of her own journey, had called to offer support.

Terry had sounded petrified, and June had offered to come visit.

Terry took her up on it immediately.

That had been yesterday, and so June had hurried to Rockerton as soon as she could.

She climbed the steps, the house on the edge of town familiar yet older.

Everything was older. Twenty years had flown by, making it seem like such a short time, and yet the house had aged, she supposed, just as much as she had.

Knocking on the door, she tried the knob; it was unlocked.

She knocked once more before she turned the knob and pushed it open, cracking it before saying, "Hello? Terry?"

"Come on in. I'm sorry. I was hurrying to get it. I was expecting you, and I put some brownies in the oven for us."

"Oh. That sounds delicious. But you didn't have to make any-thing for me."

June stepped into the entryway, closing the door behind her and turning in time to see Terry with her arms out, ready to give her a hug.

They embraced, and June felt Terry tremble. Like just that little bit of comfort was almost enough to tear down the defenses she so carefully built and expose the fear she was trying to hide.

"We can talk in the living room if you want or sit in the kitchen and smell the brownies while they cool."

"I choose the kitchen, of course," June said with a smile.

"You're a lot thinner than I remember," Terry said as they walked down the hall.

"I lost a lot of weight during chemo. Nothing tasted good. But it's so nice to smell brownies and actually feel like eating them and not throwing up."

"Is it that bad?" Terry asked, slowing and looking at June, fear all over her face.

"It wasn't terrible. I mean, there were days that were terrible, but looking back, God held my hand the whole time. I couldn't ask for anything more, and it definitely deepened my relationship with Him."

Terry nodded as they came into the kitchen, offering her a seat and pouring some tea. "I thought maybe that would be the way it would work. I know I've been in my Bible more than I ever have before. It's...scary to face the fact that you could possibly die."

"It sure is."

"Ralph has become so attentive. It's pretty obvious it scared him as well." Terry referred to her husband, and it made June smile. Sadly, because that hadn't happened to her in her relationship.

"Did you find that as well?" Terry asked with a small smile, not knowing what June had just been thinking.

June should have known that question was coming. She paused, not wanting to say anything bad about Wayne but also not wanting to lie.

Before she could say anything, Terry said, "I admired you so much, for the way that you stuck beside your husband. Your relationship with him and your determination to keep your vows were so inspiring to me."

June blinked. She had heard from other people occasionally through the years that they admired the way she treated her husband, the way she allowed him to lead their home. The way she deferred to him and never spoke ill of him.

Her own children had mentioned that at times.

But the way Terry had phrased that was so odd. The way she stuck to her vows?

"What do you mean?" June finally said.

"You know. When things went down at the company, and people found out what Wayne was doing and he was fired. You never left him. And you stood beside him so solidly. I just wasn't sure whether I would be able to do that if my husband had done the same thing."

June stared at Terry. A strange premonition came over her. Her throat tightened, and her heart felt like it was fluttering in her chest, afraid to beat, trembling.

"Why did he get fired?" she asked, her voice cracking a little on the last part of her question. Maybe it was fear.

"You know, because of that affair he was having with the insurance lady who worked at the company. They found them in his office... You didn't know?" Terry finally seemed to understand that June was in shock.

"No. I didn't know. He told me people were jealous and that's why they lied about him, and that's why he was fired."

"Oh." Terry's hand went to her mouth. There was no doubt in June's mind that Terry had not known that June didn't know. She certainly hadn't said something out of spite or unkindness. "I'm so sorry. I thought you knew. I thought you stood by him through everything."

June sat staring at her friend. She'd suspected over the years several times that Wayne was not being true to her. She'd caught a couple of text messages that didn't make sense to her, and one time, she confronted him over them.

She'd even caught him in a lie, when he told her that he never texted a woman before, but she managed to get the records from the phone company and it turned out that he had not only texted her, quite a lot, but they'd exchanged pictures on days that Wayne had had off. Wayne swore up and down that there was nothing between them, and with little kids to take care of at the time and no ability to get a job to support herself, June had chosen to believe him.

Despite the fact that she caught him in that lie.

But this. This was different. And Terry wouldn't lie to her.

"Did someone walk in on him?" she asked, wanting details but not knowing how to get them, and knowing she would probably regret knowing them

"Ralph did," Terry said, her eyes scanning June's face, almost as though she couldn't believe that June didn't know. "I'm sorry. I really am. I thought you knew."

June hugged her arms to her stomach tightly. She didn't want to break down in front of Terry. She was supposed to be here to comfort her and give her hope to get through cancer, not sit at her kitchen table, her broken heart spilling out all over the place, her chest feeling like it was going to crack, and her mind screaming that she would rather go through chemo a hundred times than face this.

Wayne had cheated.

How many times?

This was just once. Had there been more? More than the other time she caught him in a lie and accepted his explanation like it was the truth?

Were there others?

She thought back, thinking how Wayne had sounded when he had explained that people had been jealous and lied about him. He sounded so real. So honest. So believable.

She had no reason to not believe him. She hadn't suspected at all that he wasn't telling the truth. She'd felt bad for him, had comforted him and railed against the company and how unfair it was, and when he had been denied unemployment, she had wanted to fight, had been ready to march into the courtroom and fight on his behalf. It had been so wrong.

But he had told her to let it go, just not allow it to bother her. He had moved on, and she had admired that. Looking back, she had been so foolish.

But foolish wasn't the way she felt at present. Brokenhearted was more like it.

But under that pain, the pain of betrayal and of feeling like everyone around her had known what she was too stupid to see, there was relief.

After all, she had been resigned to staying with Wayne, despite the fact that he hadn't been kind to her, hadn't supported her through her cancer journey, they hadn't grown closer together, and he had never acted scared that he might lose her.

He acted irritated that she didn't have her normal energy and couldn't do the things for him that she usually did. He'd been disgusted the few times when he had to cook for himself, and he'd been downright angry when he had asked her to go pick up parts for him and she hadn't been able to because she had to go to chemo treatments.

Now, she had a business that was making money, and she had a biblical reason to divorce her husband. He had cheated. He had broken their covenant. He had not remained true to her. She could walk away.

Shaking her head, she shoved that all aside. She wanted to help her friend, not dream of divorcing her husband, so she took Terry's hand and said, "I didn't know. Thank you for telling me. I understand now why our last few interactions were a little awkward, and I couldn't figure it out, other than to think that you felt bad that my husband had been fired and your husband still had a job."

"I did feel that way. But definitely there was the awkwardness of your husband having cheated, and me not knowing what to say, since you seemed so okay with it."

"Well, I'm not okay with it, but that's not what I came here to talk about. Today is not about me, it's about you."

"You always were so very considerate of everyone around you," Terry murmured, her hands cold as they clasped June's.

"I don't know about that, but I do know that I love you, and I consider you a friend. There's no way I couldn't be here for you when you need me."

"I wasn't there for you when you got your diagnosis."

"That's okay. You didn't know. I've been in that exam room, and I've heard the word 'cancer' come out of the doctor's mouth. It's...a life-changing sentence."

"It really makes you think about your life, how you've lived it, and all of the things you wish you could go back and do better."

"It does, doesn't it?" June nodded sagely. She'd gone through all of that too. Wishing she could go back and make her life count for more. Make it count for the things that it needed to count for. The things that were important. She'd wasted so much of her life on frivolous, unnecessary, selfish things.

Not that there wasn't a time to relax, but she spent far more time worrying about herself and making sure she was taking care of everything she wanted than she had spent taking care of others.

"We don't get to redo, we just get to move forward, hopefully putting the lessons we were privileged to learn into practice."

"Privileged. Is that what cancer is? A privileged learning experience?"

"That's exactly what it is. Look at it that way. It's an opportunity to take a closer, deeper look at your life. One that you wouldn't have taken if you hadn't sat in the doctor's office and heard the C word come out of his mouth."

"I might not have much life left," Terry said, and the fear was back in her voice.

"But whatever you have left, you have the opportunity to make it count."

"That's a good way to look at it. Whatever happens, whatever time I have, I have to make good use of it."

"And there are going to be days when you don't even feel like getting out of bed. That just rolling over feels like a challenge. But you have the opportunity to praise God, no matter how you feel. Right there is your first challenge."

"You almost make me look forward to going through this. Just to see if I can rise to the challenge." There was humor now instead of fear in Terry's voice.

"It's hard. No doubt, but you're going to look back, and you're going to celebrate the victories. Realizing that it was God holding your hand helping you. Doing it for you when you couldn't do it for yourself. You let Him, and He will."

"That sounds so encouraging. I hope it's truly like that."

"It will be. And now, while you're waiting for the treatments to start, you're doing the right thing. Digging into your Bible, shoring yourself up for the times to come. I would memorize verses. I know when I was lying in bed, I wished I had more that would come to mind." June squeezed Terry's hand. "Find a good Bible app. One that reads it to you. You can play it while you lie in bed. It's not going to help you feel better, but it will remind you of all the things you can't remember on your own."

"That's such a good idea."

"It is. There are a lot of them out there, so find someone with a great voice who makes the Bible come alive. And have it so that it's not hard to find on your phone." June laughed a little. "There were times where even clicking buttons on my phone felt like a mountain too hard for me to climb."

"Really?"

"You're definitely going to have some bad days. Maybe some soothing music would help, with words and without. I didn't listen to that as much as I listened to the Bible, but there were days that helped."

"Music always helps."

"It does. Sometimes, on really bad days, I would listen to the music and wonder if I was in heaven. After all, there's supposed to be really beautiful music up there, and thinking about that makes death seem not so bad. That, and the fact that no matter what happens, whether you live or whether you die, God's love is with you, no matter what. You don't have to do it alone. You never have to do it alone."

They talked for a bit more and shared some brownies between them, reminiscing about the old days and catching up, letting each other know where their kids were and what they were doing.

Before June knew it, an hour had flown by.

"I didn't want to stay too long. I know that you have things you want to do. But I'm glad you had time to visit with me." She stood, and maybe she was wrong, but Terry looked disappointed.

"Thank you so much for coming. You really made me feel so much better. Which makes me feel worse about telling you about Wayne. I truly didn't know that you didn't know."

"I appreciate knowing. I... I don't know what I'm going to do, but I'm definitely going to do something. It's been a lot of years, but the chances are that if he did it that one time, he's done it more. I don't know that I even need to find out about any other times. I just need to figure out what God wants me to do about this time. I don't believe in mistakes, and me finding out about Wayne wasn't a mistake. I just don't know what God wants me to do about the information."

"I'll be praying for you. I... I always admired you for staying, but I couldn't fault you for leaving. After all, if Wayne lied to you, and never told you about it, and isn't asking for forgiveness now..."

He certainly wasn't. She couldn't imagine that happening, anyway. Maybe she would confront him and see what he said. If he broke down in tears, and begged her to forgive him, and asked her not to leave, maybe she'd consider staying.

As nice as that sounded, she just couldn't picture Wayne begging her to stay. She also couldn't picture him apologizing, and it was even harder to picture him admitting the truth.

She was willing to bet he would just continue to lie to her.

Lord, what do I do?

Chapter 10

Gideon parked Piper's SUV car in the grocery store lot. It was just a small store, recently opened on the edge of Sweet Water, but it should be enough to get everything on Piper's list.

"How do you guys feel about going to the park for a few minutes before we go grocery shopping?" he asked, looking in the rearview mirror at the three kids in car seats behind him.

Henry fisted his hands and put them both in the air. "Yes!"

It was so cute coming from the four-year-old that Gideon had to laugh.

Luna, possibly not understanding, clapped her hands and then imitated her brother, with a slightly less well enunciated, "Yes!"

Theodora, who definitely didn't understand, bounced in her seat and clapped her hands anyway.

"All right. It's unanimous. We're going to the playground before we get groceries."

He had thought about telling them if they were good, they'd stop afterward, but she had a few bags of frozen vegetables on her list, and he didn't want the things to get warm.

It was a nice day out, lots of sunshine with very few clouds, and temperatures in the mid-seventies.

Perfect day to play at the playground.

When he was a kid, he would have much rather gone to the playground than grocery shopping.

Regardless, he wasn't sure he was going to be able to control all three kids in the grocery store, and going to the playground first gave him a bit of a reprieve.

Not to mention, it was a beautiful day and he didn't mind going out and enjoying it a little bit.

Of course, there was a blizzard coming in two days, and he had an addition to finish on Piper's house. He couldn't tarry long.

But after what the kids had been through the last day, he figured that a little time spent at the playground would wear them out, give them a little boost, and give Piper a little bit of extra time at home to rest.

She looked tired this morning lying on the couch. The only time she'd gotten up was to go to the bathroom, using the crutches the emergency room had given her, although the doctor had told her the only time he wanted her up was for necessities.

"Are you going to play?" Henry asked as Gideon got him unbuckled and then worked on Luna.

"Of course. That's what playgrounds are for, isn't it?" He gave Henry a look that said anybody who thought he wasn't going to play on the playground was crazy.

"You're too big!" Henry said, putting his little hands on his hips and giving Gideon a very adult-like look.

"Well, am I too big to fit or too big to play?" Because there was a difference.

"Both."

Maybe there wasn't a difference.

"How about let's see. If I fit, I can play, right?"

"I don't think the big people are allowed to play on the playground. It's just for little people," Henry said, watching as Gideon set Luna to the side, telling her to stay put, and started working on Theodora.

Piper had supervised him packing a baby bag, and he shouldered that, then picked Luna up and put her on his shoulders before he grabbed Theodora and put her on his opposite hip.

"Sorry, buddy. I can't carry you too. You're going to have to walk."

"That's all right. I'm used to it." Henry shrugged his narrow little shoulders and skipped along beside Gideon as they walked toward the playground.

Henry ran immediately to the monkey bars while Gideon put Theodora in a baby swing before lifting Luna down off his shoulders.

She didn't want to follow her brother to the monkey bars but was content for him to put her in a swing right beside Theodora. He stood between the two of them and pushed them gently.

If only he could have them so contained in the grocery store. He figured he would put one in the cart, facing him. But what was he going to do with the other one? Would she ride in the cart? Would she try to climb out?

Henry would probably be fine to walk along beside.

He still hadn't quite gotten everything figured out in his head, wishing he had at least a little bit of experience with kids, which would have been really helpful around about now, when Miss April walked over from the grocery store parking lot.

He hadn't seen her park, but he recognized her right away as she made her way over.

"Good morning. What a night you had last night," Miss April said as she got closer.

"It was definitely interesting," Gideon said. "I appreciate you coming. That really eased Piper's mind that there were people she trusted watching her children."

"Any time. It wasn't a hardship. It's been a while since I was out that late, though. And I had to explain to my husband that I was watching children, not running around on him."

Gideon laughed, figuring that Miss April's husband wasn't the slightest bit worried about her running around on him.

"How was Piper doing this morning? Was she in a lot of pain?"

"She had some, but I think as long as she stays off it and keeps it elevated, she's going to do just fine."

When he left, the last thing he said to her was that she needed to start calling people to cancel the appointments she had scheduled for today.

Come to think of it, she hadn't agreed to that. The thought made him antsy.

"That's good to hear. Sometimes breaks hurt so much that the pain keeps you up and you can't sleep. Piper, as much as she has going on, needs to rest."

"All she's going to have going on for a while is watching her children. She's not allowed to be standing for any length of time, and she's to stay off it as much as she can."

"She's not going to be able to work?"

"No. And that's something I needed to talk to you about." Gideon hadn't thought about it much, but with Miss April standing in front of him and the idea in his head, he just said, "I think the town needs to do something for her. She's not going to be able to make a living for her family for at least four weeks, and that's if everything goes well and the doctor gives the okay once her foot has started to heal. Still, it's going to be very hard for her."

Miss April smiled, almost the way a Sunday school teacher would smile at a bright child in her class. "I'm already on it. I'm meeting my friends at the community center in just a few minutes, and we're going to find a man for Piper to marry. It's not going to be an easy task, considering she has six children, but we know several older widowers who might be interested in supporting her if she would be willing to take care of their house and keep them company."

Gideon froze, staring at Miss April.

He was so shocked, Theodora almost hit him as her swing came back toward him. He put his hand out just in time, giving her a half-hearted push and managing to get his mouth shut before he looked back at Miss April.

"You're trying to find someone to marry her?" he said, feeling stupid, because Miss April hadn't stuttered. That's exactly what she had said.

"That seems to be the best long-term solution. The town is already helping her a good bit. Although you're donating your time, we bought materials for her addition. I'm not saying she's not deserving of more help, it just seems like a husband would be a win-win solution for everyone. The children would get a father, a widower who is lonely and in need of companionship would have a wife, and Piper would have security for herself and her family. I don't see any downsides." Miss April nodded her head as though to confirm her words.

"You said 'older widower.' Piper can't be more than thirty or thirty-five. How old do you mean?" Gideon asked, trying to imagine Piper with anyone.

He couldn't even picture her with Baker or even Zeke, both of whom were unmarried and much more Piper's age than some "older" widower.

"There are several who are sixty or sixty-five, and that's not too old. Especially for a second marriage for them. We have one who's in his later fifties. I was thinking about him a good deal. Although his wife had some complaints about him when she divorced him, which were never proven. All hearsay."

"Complaints?"

"He had some addictions," Miss April said sadly, shaking her head.

Immediately Gideon thought of porn. And of Piper and her six children. Whether the rumor about the addictions was true or not, any of the other men could have addictions as well. Or they could be mean. As well as much older than Piper. If she were in her fifties, it wouldn't be so bad, but to marry a man twice her age?

"Can you find someone her age?" Gideon finally asked.

Miss April laughed. "It seems that as quickly as unmarried men come into town, they get snatched up." She sighed. "And this isn't something we can wait around on. Piper is in some dire straits, especially if she can't work. We can't take the time to finesse this. We need to get it done now."

"I agree with that. She definitely needs help, and she needs it soon." He didn't want to disclose Piper's financial situation to Miss April. She didn't seem like a gossip. She had mentioned one man's addiction, but he had no idea who she was talking about, and she had stated flat-out that it could be just a rumor.

He was impressed that she hadn't tried to bend his ear or spread rumors that could be false.

Still, Piper's financial situation wasn't his information to share, so he didn't.

He spoke with Miss April a little bit more before she told him she needed to head out and walked slowly away.

By that time, Henry was at the swings too, pushing himself on a bigger swing, just down the way from where Gideon pushed Luna and Theodora.

If he noticed that Gideon wasn't quite as happy or talkative as he had been when they arrived at the playground, Henry didn't say.

Gideon tried to pay attention to the kids and answer their questions, chatting like he pictured their mom doing, but his mind was whirling.

Just because Piper had six children didn't mean she couldn't find a man who was worthy of her.

And not that a widower would be a terrible match, just...the age difference was so great. She'd end up taking care of her children, and by the time she was done with that, she'd be providing nursing care for an elderly man who also happened to be her husband.

She deserved a better life than that.

At least he wanted her to have one. He wanted her to have the fun and happiness that everyone craved.

She'd already been through the death of her husband, and the financial situation that looked so bleak had to be weighing down on her as well. And then to break her foot on top of it all... It seemed like she couldn't catch a break. Was nothing good ever going to happen to her?

Of course, the town was pitching in and put an addition on her house, but she had lived in a two-bedroom home with six children for two years. And in the small amount of time that he'd spent with her, he'd never heard her complain. In fact, when he arrived to put the addition on, she had said she didn't want charity.

It wasn't like she was expecting people to help her. He had to admire that, but at the same time, he wanted more for her. More than constant serving, constant having people need her, never having time for her to take a breath and be able to relax.

Maybe the ladies would pick a good man.

And maybe they wouldn't.

As he got Luna out of her swing and set her down so he could get Theodora out of hers, Henry hopped out of his swing and came over and stood beside Gideon.

"Are you gonna let that lady find an old man for Mommy?"

Gideon stared down at him. He hadn't thought Henry was listening. Even if he had known, he wasn't sure he would have been careful about what he said, since he would think that the kid would be happy to have a dad, but maybe there had been something in his tone. Regardless, the eyes that Henry looked up at him with were worried, his brow furrowed.

"Your mommy might not want her to. But I know that your mommy is going to make sure that he's the right man."

Gideon didn't know any such thing, but just from the time he spent around Piper, he guessed that's the way she would respond. Her children would come first.

But he could only imagine it would be tempting to her to marry anyone who offered, no matter how old they were, just for the security it would provide for her children.

Sixty wasn't that old. Not anymore.

That's when he realized that it wasn't the potential suitors' age that bothered him. It was the idea that he couldn't imagine any other man with Piper.

Or maybe he just didn't think anyone was good enough.

The grocery store wasn't quite as hard as what he thought it was going to be, and while he did miss two items on her list, rice and beans, he wasn't sure whether it was a deliberate oversight, or whether he really didn't see them.

Regardless, as he checked the list while he was sitting in the parking lot, he decided he was not going to go back in for them. Rather, the kids seemed like they were getting hungry, and Theodora kept rubbing her eyes which he assumed meant she was getting tired.

Piper hadn't said what time her nap would be or even if she took one, but he hadn't told her that he was going to stop at the playground, so Piper might have expected him home by now.

Regardless, it only took ten minutes to drive to Piper's house and pull into her driveway.

There was another car parked beside his pickup, and he assumed that someone was already coming to visit her. He was a little annoyed, because he wanted Piper to get some rest, but maybe they had brought food, and if they had, he appreciated it. It would be one less meal that he would need to cook.

And what was he doing assuming that he was going to be taking care of her?

The thought came to him as he was opening his door.

When had he gone from being someone who just happened to be there to being someone who had taken the responsibility on his own shoulders? He wasn't sure. The idea bothered him.

But rather than dwelling on it, he shoved the thought aside. Determined to be thankful for the town and not be so protective of Piper and so concerned about her health and rest.

His determination lasted until he walked in the door, Luna on his shoulders, Theodora in one arm, five grocery bags in the other hand, while Henry carried one in each hand.

It was going to take another two trips to finish emptying the car, but they had made a good dent in it.

He totally forgot about the groceries though, when he stepped in the door and saw a lady he recognized from church sitting in a kitchen chair, with Piper standing behind her, putting her hair in curlers.

Chapter 11

"You're not supposed to be up," Gideon said as a welcome when he walked in the door.

Piper glanced up, trying to not show her heart was beating hard and her hands were sweating.

She gave him a half smile and shrugged her shoulders. "I have too many people who are counting on me. I can't just go and cancel on everyone."

She needed the money. But she couldn't say that in front of Mrs. Steinbeck.

Gideon had been very clear about his desire for her to rest, to obey the doctor's orders, but she had not agreed to his demand when he left and had every intention of working all day.

Despite the fact that her foot was already burning with pain.

It was impossible to cut hair and keep the crutches under her arm, and she couldn't stand in one spot, since she didn't have a chair that spun.

Even if she did, some movement would be required.

She didn't begrudge the fact that she didn't have the necessary equipment, because she had learned that saying "if only" was a waste of time.

If only she had a beautician's chair.

If only she hadn't broken her foot.

If only she had enough money to buy groceries and pay her bills.

If only her husband hadn't died.

Nothing would change any of those things. And she suspected that as her life played out, eventually she wouldn't want it to. Although the idea that she would ever be able to see the reasoning behind her husband dying seemed impossible, she knew God had a plan for her life.

Richard's accident had caused her to grow up. Quite a lot. And it had driven her closer to the Lord.

She had had to get her anxiety in check, her fear of the future, to shut out the worst-case scenarios which played out in her head at night when she lay down. She had had to give that all over to the Lord. Otherwise she would have gone crazy, and she wouldn't have been able to raise her children.

Knowing that trusting in the Lord was the only thing that she could do to keep herself sane, she had thrown herself into that.

Still, God didn't just hand her things, He wanted her to work for them.

And that was why she was up, cutting hair.

"The doctor told you to stay off that foot." Gideon sounded like his words came out through clenched teeth.

"And I'm not on that foot. I'm standing on the other one." Her words were said simply, and she was happy to note that there was no tremor in them, despite the fact that her hands were trembling.

She kept a confident smile on her face though as she continued to work on Mrs. Steinbeck's hair.

"He told you to stay off your feet. I took the children so you could rest, not so you could work."

"Thank you. I appreciate it. I didn't ask you to do it, though." She looked at him finally, a challenge on her face.

The anger in his eyes surprised her. She barely knew him, and yet, he truly was angry that she was up.

"The doctor said if that doesn't heal right, you won't stand without pain again. That will affect your income for the rest of your life. Are you willing to take that chance?"

"I don't have a choice." She said her words as firmly as she could, willing him to understand that while the doctor's way might be the best way, her way was the only way that would work. It was the only way that would put food on her table. It was the only way that would pay the mortgage in order to keep her children under the roof with her. It was the only way that would keep her mother out of her house, if that was even possible, which she highly doubted, since she had texted her this morning to let her know what had happened.

Her mother had responded and not said anything about coming, but it wouldn't surprise Piper at all for her to show up later this afternoon. It would be her way.

If Piper had any extra time at all, she would be cleaning her house. That would be the first thing her mother would start complaining about.

Gideon, his arms crossed, his feet planted, stared her down.

She refused to drop her gaze, staring right back at him. He knew that she couldn't even afford the groceries he was bringing into her home. He knew she needed to be up working.

She wasn't arguing about whether or not he was right. She wasn't even arguing about whether or not the doctor was right. She would happily admit that they were both correct.

But she didn't have a choice about who she was going to listen to and what she was going to do.

Finally, his lips pressed tight together, a muscle working on the side of his jaw, and a vein bulging in his temple, Gideon turned, said something low to Henry, and the two of them walked back outside.

She assumed they'd be coming back in with more groceries.

Normally she didn't have enough money to buy everything she put on her list, but she figured with the storm coming and with Gideon offering, she would do what needed to be done.

"Gideon always seemed like such a fun guy. I've never seen him angry before," Mrs. Steinbeck said, her hand fluttering up by her chest, as though Gideon had scared her.

He was angry, but it wasn't violently angry. He wasn't even yelling angry. And he was angry because he cared about her.

That gave her pause.

He cared. Why else would he be upset that she was standing and working?

And she had to appreciate the fact that he had enough self-control not to yell at her in front of her client.

He hadn't even argued with her. She appreciated that.

She wasn't thinking that she wasn't going to hear anything more from him, but she figured he wasn't going to be saying it in front of people.

That was a relief.

She was correct in her assumption, and while she missed their easy camaraderie of the evening before, where they were joking and laughing, he still took care of the children, putting Theodora to bed and taking Henry and Luna out to the addition with him while he worked steadily until almost one o'clock.

She was sweeping up hair from Frederick Jones, who had come in for his monthly trim, and was keeping an eye on the driveway for Stephanie Plummer, who had been supposed to arrive at one o'clock, and also for her mom.

As soon she got the hair swept up, she would start on the dishes in the sink, wishing she had enough time to take her long-handled brush and swipe the cobwebs in the corners of her living room. Her mother was sure to see those. And comment about all the terrible things that spiders did to people. She'd probably get the lowdown on the number of people who were killed every year in the United States by spider bites and the cost of hospitalization as well.

Her mother was a bit of a neat freak.

But she meant well.

"Are you going to go lie down now?" Gideon said as he walked into the kitchen, in his stocking feet, Luna on one hip, Henry trotting along beside him.

Henry seemed to have really taken to him, which was interesting, since Henry was her kid who usually hung back.

"No. Once I get this hair swept up, if Stephanie hasn't come, I'm going to go start the dishes, and if I manage to get those done, I'm going to work on getting the cobwebs down in the living room. I'm sure my mother will be here any minute."

"So you told her?"

She had mentioned last night that she would wait and text her mom in the morning. Not just because she was already in bed, but because Piper knew it was going to be a difficult conversation.

"I did. She would have been more upset with me the longer I waited, so I knew I had to." She shrugged, missing the banter, missing the friendly Gideon. Not liking this glowering, disapproving, almost angry man who had taken his place.

"And she's coming?"

"She didn't say she was, but she never does. She just shows up. And it'll be easier for me to clean than it will be for me to listen to her complain that I haven't."

"Why don't you let me handle your mom."

She flipped her hair back over her shoulder and looked up at Gideon. "I appreciate all of your help. I really appreciate the groceries. I appreciate you being here yesterday and taking me to the hospital. You don't owe me anything. In fact, it's me that owes you. And I don't like it. You don't have to stay here, and you don't have to keep helping me, and you definitely don't have to boss me around. And beyond that, I can handle my own mother."

She didn't know why she was feeling so defensive. Maybe because he was butting in, and he had no right. He had no dog in this fight, she barely even knew him before yesterday.

"I guess you're right. Here's the kids. They're hungry."

"You can stay." That came out with more anger than she meant for it to.

"No. This is your life. You can handle it."

That wasn't what she wanted. She sighed, blowing her breath out and closing her eyes. Why was she so stupid sometimes? Her prickly pride caused her to shove people away when they were only trying to help.

"Wait."

Gideon took two more steps before he stopped. But he didn't turn around.

"I'm sorry. I'm sorry. I'm sorry."

She didn't even know what else to say. She was on the verge of tears, and she didn't know where they were even coming from. She had started the day out so strong. Maybe it was because her foot hurt, her hip hurt, her arms were tired, and everything was sore from the position she had to take trying to keep her foot up and her weight on the other one. Unaccustomed to such an awkward way to stand, her whole body ached. Plus, she was hungry, she had to find something for her children to eat, and her mother was coming.

On top of that, she had a whole afternoon of clients.

When he set Luna down, she hurried over to her mom and was now holding onto Piper's leg, which normally Piper barely noticed, but with trying to keep her broken foot off the ground, it threw her off balance, and she might have been able to catch herself, but as she put her broken foot down, an automatic reaction that she did without thinking, pain shot up through her leg and felt like it exploded out her elbows, turning her world red.

She yelped as her ribs hit the countertop, and she fell forward.

Thankfully, she missed her children and didn't land on top of either one of them, but seeing their mother fall had both Luna and Theodora bursting into tears.

Their cries drowned out the sound of Gideon's footsteps, but she felt his touch on her shoulder and heard his muttered, "Stubborn,

stubborn woman," as his hands came around her back and her knees, and he lifted her up.

"I suppose if you break the other leg, we'll be going to the ER, where they'll tell you to stay off it, too, and then you'll come home and promptly stand on your head in order to cut hair." His words were muttered as he carried her to the couch.

"Thank you for asking me how I am. I don't think I broke my other foot, but my ribs hurt."

"Are you due for another pain pill?"

"At one o'clock."

"We have fifteen minutes. I think we'll take it early. Where are they?"

"I can't tell you. You'll steal them." Her eyes were closed, and the words came out around the pain that still throbbed all through her body, but she couldn't help the lifting of her lips.

Gideon, who had been pushing himself to his feet after kneeling to lay her on the couch, froze. She could feel his presence just hovering over her.

"No. You are not allowed to be funny and cute and make me laugh. I'm angry, and I'm going to stay that way. So quit it."

But his words lacked any of the heat that they'd had since he'd come home and seen her standing, working. And she could hear the humor in them as well.

That made her smile.

"What are you gonna do? Break my other foot?"

"I am sorely tempted to. Sorely tempted."

"I think there are laws against that."

"I think, when a man is dealing with a woman as stubborn as you are, he stops caring about laws and starts thinking about other things."

"Other things?" She lifted her brows, without opening her eyes. "Like breaking feet?"

"I was thinking more along the lines of kissing you. It's the only way I know how to handle someone as stubborn as you are. And even then, I'm not completely sure it would work."

Kissing her?

"You've been angry at me all day."

"Because sometime between yesterday and today, I started to care about you. A lot. And it's frustrating that you don't seem to care about yourself, at all."

"Kissing me?" She cracked one eye and looked up at him. Really? Did he really say that?

She knew she was pathetic. Here she was with the broken foot, ribs that felt like they might be broken too, bills she couldn't pay, groceries she couldn't afford, and six—count them, six—kids, and yet all she could think about was the idea that this man, funny and compassionate, kind and selfless, who seemed to be really good with her kids, had been thinking about kissing her.

"You are not supposed to be smiling right now," he said, but there was absolutely no censure or anger left in his tone, and it sounded a lot like the Gideon from last night.

"So...today, so far, is that the way you always are when you're angry?" she asked, a little smile hovering around the corners of her lips. She knew she had more pressing things to do, but they all seemed to fade in the background as she waited for Gideon to answer her.

"I don't know. I honestly can't remember the last time I was angry. I certainly haven't been that angry in a really, *really* long time. Like, since I was two and threw a howling, screaming hissy fit when my mom tried to sit me on Santa Claus's lap. And I only know I was that angry because they told me. I was too little to remember."

"Santa Claus. I'm so glad you chose your battles wisely."

"Someone has to fight against jolly old St. Nicholas who tries to push Jesus out of the picture at Christmastime. I was doing my part as a two-year-old."

"Wow. So that was your last angry fit, railing against Santa Claus, and then the single mom with six kids and a broken foot trying to earn a living...I was the next person to throw you into a rage. Interesting."

"Stop saying it like that. You make me sound ridiculous."

"That's because you are." She didn't say that with any heat, but with a smile, and he took it exactly the way she meant it.

"Really? I'm ridiculous for wanting you to listen to the doctor? For wanting to take care of you, after I admitted that I cared for you? Is this the way you treat everyone who cares for you?"

That question made Piper snap her mouth closed.

She had been dreading her mother's visit, but her mother cared for her. Truly. She did.

She complained about the dirty house, just because she was concerned about her grandchildren not being raised in a clean environment. It didn't matter how many times Piper told her that dirt was good for children's immune systems, and children who were raised in dirty homes were much less likely to develop allergies than children who were not, but her mother didn't listen, which frustrated Piper.

"I'm sorry. I think I hit a sore spot," Gideon said, dropping to his knee again beside Piper.

"I haven't had too many people ask me that. Actually, I'm not sure anyone ever has. But...you're right. You were angry because you cared about me, and I knew that when I was standing in the kitchen, but I still wasn't very nice. And none of my thoughts about my mother have been very nice either, even though I know she'll be here because she cares, and if she gives me a hard time, it's because she cares as well."

"I came down pretty heavy-handed on you. I... I guess I felt like what I was saying was common sense, and you should do it just because. I am more of a rule follower than maybe I seem sometimes, and I felt like you should be following the rules as well, that common sense dictated you should."

"Sometimes common sense doesn't pay the bills," she mumbled.

"I guess I've never been in the position where common sense didn't. But...you would know."

"Unfortunately, that's true. I do know." She closed her eyes, then opened them, as Luna and Theodora stood on either side of Gideon, begging to be picked up. Theodora still had tears streaking down her face, but both of them had quit crying some time ago. "That's still no excuse. Especially when someone who cares about me was willing to make the sacrifice to take care of me, and I rather rudely shoved you aside."

"I think we both admitted that we were wrong. And both of us could have done better. Agreed?"

Unless she was mistaken, the expression on his face was rather hopeful. Hopeful that they could come to a truce, or maybe an understanding, that both of them could go forward, trying to do better.

"I agree. Especially about me. I'm sorry. I'm sorry I allowed my pride to get in the way."

"Mine too. My bossiness and thinking that I knew best, and my unwillingness to understand that your experience was driving your actions, which made perfect sense to you, even though they seemed crazy to me."

"Yeah. I suppose a lot of the things I do would seem crazy to you."

"Six kids is crazy. But I actually enjoyed this morning with the kids. They keep things interesting, and you're never lacking for company."

"It's an extrovert's dream, I suppose."

"That's me."

He didn't need to tell her that he was an extrovert. It was obvious. She smiled. She had more introvert tendencies, but as a mom of six, she didn't have time to indulge herself.

"Now, are you gonna tell me where those pain pills are so I can shove half of them in my pocket, or not?"

She told him, laughing as she did so. And he went, getting the pills and a glass of water and bringing them back to her.

"I think the laughter helps just as much as the pain pills," she said as he put the pills into her hand and then helped her sit up with the hand that wasn't holding Theodora while she took the water from him and swallowed the pills.

"I read studies where they put laughter head-to-head with pain pills, and it does better than you think."

"I guess God knew what he was doing when he sent you to me then," she said, handing him the glass back, her eyes still pinched with pain, but her lips curved up.

"Or maybe he sent you to me, to show me that I'm not nearly as humble as I need to be and that maybe I'm a little quick to judge and too slow to see my own faults."

She shook her head no but didn't say anything more. The pain throbbed up her legs and wrapped around her stomach. It exhausted her.

She loved it though. Loved that he was taking the blame. That he could see where he needed to improve. That he wasn't pointing fingers at her and telling her how wrong she was. Even though she *was* wrong. She supposed that was the way most arguments were, either side could give in some.

The problem was, often one wouldn't give in without knowing the other would too. She was that way. She didn't want to admit she was wrong without having someone else admit it as well.

Again, he'd been willing to do that, with no guarantee that she was going to follow suit.

"Give me one more minute to rest, then I'll call the clients I have this afternoon and tomorrow and cancel them all. I've already canceled the ones from Thursday on, because of the storm."

He didn't say anything, and then she heard the glass clank on the table beside her and felt movement as he knelt beside her, and then his rough hand covered hers.

It was warm and hard, but it cradled her fingers tenderly.

"I'd appreciate it if you do that. I... I'd really like to see you take care of yourself. And I'd like to help you if you'll let me."

His words were humble, soft, not the commanding tone of earlier.

"I'll let you."

Chapter 12

By the time Gideon had the kids fed and put to bed for their afternoon naps, Piper was fast asleep on the couch.

She hadn't even eaten.

Gideon watched her sleep for just a few minutes, thinking about their earlier argument and kind of amazed at how angry he had been.

He hadn't been lying when he said he couldn't ever remember being that angry before.

Anger was an emotion he didn't usually have to deal with.

It was odd.

He used the drill to sink another screw when his phone buzzed in his pocket.

> **I have your clothes and the stuff you asked for. Where you at?**

> Come around back.

Baker wouldn't have any trouble finding him. And there was no need for him to go through the house.

Indeed, just thirty seconds later, Baker stepped through the doorway that was framed but didn't have a door hung.

"Are you going to have the roof on before the snow hits?" Baker asked as he stepped inside, carrying his duffel which looked like it was stuffed full. He probably packed a lot more than what Gideon had asked for.

The thought made Gideon grin.

"I hope to. I guess we'll see how things go."

He hadn't wanted to do any work where anything might fall down and hit the kids, so he had done things out of his usual order.

"I'd like to work with you for a bit if you want me to," Baker said, throwing the duffel down by the door into the house and grabbing a battery off the charger, slapping it into the drill that sat beside it.

"I'd appreciate it," Gideon said, knowing Baker was a great guy to work with.

He had a good head on his shoulders and the kind of brain that could figure problems out and didn't need a lot of instruction.

Baker had told him that he had done terribly in school, not necessarily because he wasn't smart, but because he hadn't been able to sit still.

He was one of those people who had joined the military in order to keep himself out of prison. Figuring that he needed the rules and regulation and being forced into doing what he was commanded to do.

It had been an excellent decision on his part, and Gideon didn't know too many men who had the character and integrity Baker did.

"You know the ladies in town are trying to marry that girl off," Baker said about five minutes later, after they'd settled into a rhythm, working on getting the last of the trusses screwed in before they started putting on the roof.

"I did. I heard that in town when I was shopping this morning, but I'm kinda surprised you heard it."

"All right. We're going to have to talk about the shopping stuff in a minute, but Miss April actually called me."

"Miss April called you?" Gideon asked, pausing from where he stood near the top of the ladder he had leaning against a two-by-four.

"Yeah. Apparently she's cold-calling guys, looking for a husband for Piper, and to my knowledge, she hasn't found one yet, but she's looking pretty hard."

"It's kind of interesting that she didn't say anything to me about it." Gideon murmured the words out loud, not meaning that he wanted to, just meaning that he had spoken with her, and she'd only talked about trying to find older men.

"I asked her the same thing. Why she wasn't asking you."

"How do you know she didn't?"

"Because I figured you'd take her up on it."

Gideon grunted, but he didn't say anything.

"She said that she wasn't going to ask you, because you'd been here, saw how chaotic it was, and there was no way you'd agree to marry Piper and put yourself in a situation like this." Baker laughed. "That was after I told her no. Obviously, since she was trying to talk me into it before that, but after I declined, four times if I recall correctly, she admitted that I was wise to do so."

That made Gideon angry. The idea that Miss April herself would think that it would take deceit and a man who didn't know what he was getting into in order to get him to take Piper. Didn't she know that Piper was an amazing woman who deserved a husband who thought the world of her? And the kids, at least Henry, Luna, and Theodora, since those were the three he'd hung around the most, certainly deserved to have a wonderful dad. And they weren't crazy, there were just a lot of them. They were good kids. They listened well and hadn't even been that hard to go grocery shopping with, which had been a pleasant surprise for Gideon.

"You look angry. I don't think I've ever seen you angry."

"Funny, since this is the second time today I've been angry. But you're right. Until that point in my life, I can't remember being angry before."

"What makes you angry about that?"

"Because Piper's a good woman. She's sweet and funny, she works hard, and yeah, she's as stubborn as a three-foot-in-diameter tree stump stuck in the ground, but other than that, she really doesn't have any bad qualities."

"Sounds like she's as stubborn as you are."

"Prideful was more like it. That's my issue." Gideon didn't say anything more about that. Baker didn't need to hear all about his faults. He knew them well enough.

"Think that's probably an issue with most men," Baker murmured instead, and Gideon had to agree. He wouldn't have considered himself prideful, but that's what it was when he expected people to see things his way, when he thought they were crazy for doing things their way instead. When he expected them to listen to him and got offended when they didn't. Even if it was because he cared about them.

"So, are you just going to let Miss April call around and offer her to anyone who will take her?"

He didn't like to be pushed like that. Like it was somehow his fault that Miss April was calling people.

"What do you propose I do to stop it?" Gideon said, sinking the screw into the board with a satisfying shove of the drill.

"You're here. You apparently went shopping with her kids today, which you still haven't explained to me—"

"I don't owe you an explanation."

"And you're all testy, which is really weird."

"It is, isn't it?" He didn't like it. Didn't like the grumpiness that seemed to have descended upon him when it came to Piper.

He liked the laughing and the joking they'd done the night before. Not the way he got all huffy every time someone didn't treat her the way he thought they should.

"So, in addition to putting on an addition for her, apparently you're doing her shopping as well? Babysitting her kids?"

"Quit pushing me," he said, his words short.

"You never have a problem pushing other people."

"I joke with them. I don't shove them into a corner and try to trap them into saying what I want them to say."

"What do you think I want you to say?"

"That I'm packing up and leaving?"

"Not at all. I just brought your clothes. You're packing up and staying. Or packing up and leaving us to move in with her apparently. I just don't think you want to do that without a ring."

"Don't be ridiculous. It's supposed to snow. If I'm going to be stuck somewhere, I might as well be stuck here, working on her addition, which is sorely needed by the way. The woman's been sleeping on the couch for the last two years."

"Really? I'm sure there's a lot of people in a lot worse situations, interesting that you seem to be stuck on this one."

"So you're telling me that I shouldn't be helping her?"

"No, I'm saying the ladies in town are trying to get her married off. You are apparently moving in, doing her shopping, babysitting her kids, and building her addition... Why don't you marry her?"

Gideon worked in silence, thankfully doing work that he'd been doing all his life and he didn't have to think about it much because Baker had just said exactly what he'd been thinking.

Except, when he thought it, it sounded crazy. The idea of marrying someone he barely knew. How would he even approach her about that? *Hey, everyone in town thinks you need to get married, so want to do it with me?*

It was crazy. The dumbest idea he'd ever had.

"By the way, what's up with that steer that's out there? Isn't that the steer that runs around Sweet Water?"

"Yeah. I stopped at the feed store and bought some feed and treats for it, since it seems to be parking itself right here."

"I guess you know there's a rumor about that steer going around town."

"I know. I've lived here longer than you have, remember?"

"I'm just saying." Baker lifted his hands in innocence and then kept working.

Gideon didn't say anything more, but he knew the rumors about Billy. He was supposed to be a matchmaking steer.

People had been flocking to the diner because of the Marry Me Chicken, and they had been staying around town because of Billy and Munchy. So far, the pig hadn't shown up, but Munchy was more the object of the steer's affection than a participator in the matchmaking schemes of the steer.

At least according to the lore of the townspeople.

It was all a bunch of baloney as far as Gideon was concerned. He just felt bad for the steer because while the grass had started to grow, it was still pretty short. He didn't want Billy to starve to death.

"Somebody's going to be dropping a bale of hay off later, but I got some grain and a few treats the kids can feed it. I've seen that it's good with children, even though those horns look wicked."

"They've used it as part of the petting zoo during different town festivals. The kids should be safe."

"Yeah. I don't think I'll let them do it without supervision though. You can't be too careful."

"Where is Gideon Marsh? What have you done with my friend?"

Gideon's head jerked up from where he was measuring a board.

He was going to ask Baker what he was talking about, but he knew. He wasn't exactly known for being overly cautious or protective. He was known as the goof-off. The one who was never serious. The one who was levelheaded and never got upset.

He kept working. There was no good answer for that.

He felt protective of Piper and her children. Like it was somehow his responsibility to take care of them. He couldn't really explain where the feeling came from. After all, it wasn't like he knew her or that he had even been friends with her for that long.

"Listen, all I know is someone's going to end up marrying her. I just kinda figured I would tell you about it today while I was here, but after seeing you, seeing how you're acting, listening to you, I kind of feel like...it should be you."

"I'm not exactly the kind of person who is mature enough to be a father to six kids. To be responsible for providing for them and taking care of them. You remember why Erin broke up with me."

"Man, that was, like, six years ago. You've changed since then."

Gideon didn't say anything. He had changed since then, but not that dramatically.

Lord?

He'd barely questioned God when a verse from his childhood came into his head. **When he hath tried me, I shall come forth as gold.**

Erin's breakup and the soul-searching he'd done after that had changed him. Had he really grown that much?

"Maybe God's plan for your life is that He would use the kids and Piper to grow you into the man he wants you to become. I don't think He's expecting you to start out as a perfect person, as nice as that would be for Piper and her kids."

"Well, they're sure not getting anyone perfect in me," he mumbled.

Could Baker be right? Was that what he was here for? This woman and her children?

He'd never considered marrying a woman with children before. In fact, seeing that a woman had kids had caused him to turn away. He might have considered someone with one or two, but six?

"Maybe I wanted to have children of my own." He didn't know where that thought came from, but he put it out there.

"And maybe you will," Baker said easily.

"To have more kids when we already have six? That's nuts."

"Is it? You've always loved people. You've always loved happy chaos, laughing and joking and having fun. Isn't that what a big family is all about?"

"That would be a really big family."

"And we're getting our dude ranch started. There'll be plenty of work for everyone, and there should be money streams coming in from the different things that we've done, the cows, the crop dusting, the dude ranch itself, and who knows what else. Your kids wouldn't have a better place to grow up."

"I can't disagree with that." He had been excited about the dude ranch. The things that they were doing out on Sweet Briar, the plans they had, and the things they wanted to grow and develop.

But he hadn't considered doing that with six children alongside of him...and a wife.

He could hardly picture him married, let alone the father of six kids.

"Why don't you think about it? Pray about it. If this is something that God wants you to do, I think you'll feel at peace about it, even if there is still fear whenever you take your first steps."

"I'm not even sure I want to pray about it. I think Piper's pretty awesome, and I love her kids, but...I've only known her for two days."

"And you've seen her at her worst. Right? You just had a broken leg. You know how much that hurts, and we saw how grumpy you got."

"I wasn't grumpy," he said, and he sounded testy, even to his own ears.

"Just like that," Baker said, nodding at him like that proved he had been grumpy with his broken leg.

But Baker had made his point. Breaking a bone hurt, and Piper had not only broken two bones, but she was facing an impending blizzard unable to buy food for her kids, and she hadn't been mean or grumpy or unkind. Except when he tried to force her into not working, not realizing that he had been scaring her because he had been asking her to quit doing the livelihood which fed her children and kept a roof over their heads.

He understood that a little better now, and at the same time, it dawned on him what a huge sacrifice it had been for her to agree to his terms. To call all the people and cancel.

For Piper, that had been a major step of faith. And she had done it because he had asked her to. If he hadn't, she would still be standing in the kitchen right now doing people's hair.

He might be able to, if not "save" her, at least make her life a little easier.

Baker and he started talking about the dude ranch, and he didn't say anything more about Piper, and Gideon didn't bring her up either, although he did go in several times to check on the children, to see if they had woken up.

They slept long enough for Baker and him to get the roof on and all the sides enclosed, although they didn't get the windows and doors in before Baker left.

He promised to come back the next day and give him a hand with that, and then Gideon should be able to finish all the plumbing and wiring and carpentry work on the inside.

After Baker left, Gideon went in in time to see Henry coming out of his room, rubbing his eyes.

He checked to see it was almost time for the bus. He figured Alice would help with the little kids, and Lucas would probably work outside with him.

His eyes moved from the sleepy Henry, who was working his way toward the couch where Piper still lay. Her eyes blinked, having that glazed look of someone who was just waking up.

It looked like the pain pills had kicked in, because her face wasn't pinched, and she seemed relaxed, although she blinked a few times like she didn't quite recognize him.

She looked like a little girl, definitely not like a mom of six kids. She was adorable, and he smiled.

That was just before the door burst open, and the most fearsome woman he'd ever seen stepped inside the house.

Chapter 13

Piper blinked. She'd been having the nicest dream. A dream where she was in a field of daisies, the kids were all clean, miraculously, since a bubbling brook flowed through the field, providing background music as her children laughed and played, chasing each other and not fighting at all. Not even a little.

She reclined on a blanket, eating the most delicious picnic food she'd ever eaten in her entire life and somehow knowing that she had made it that morning, although she didn't remember doing so. But the thing that made the dream so much different than any other dream she'd ever had was that Richard wasn't the man sitting across from her.

He might have been gone for two years, but still she dreamed of him occasionally, and when she pictured her family, he was always there. Of course she knew those thoughts were just pipe dreams, since Richard would never come back, but when she was asleep, she couldn't control the direction of her thoughts, and Richard always smiled benevolently at her, complimenting her cooking and telling her how beautiful she was.

Today, there hadn't been a man across from her. He had been sitting, holding her shoulders in his lap, his arms around her, pulling her close. They had been talking and laughing, and when his hands threaded through hers and she looked up into his face, it had been Gideon and not Richard.

That was about the time she heard the door open and blinked, trying to push the dream away and come back to reality as Gideon stood in the house, looking down at her with a bemused look on his face. A little different than the look that had been on his face in the dream, where his eyes had been dark, hooded, and his breath fanned her cheek when he kissed her temple.

Still, the man standing across the room from her looked at her like she was cute and not a total mess.

That was a miracle in itself, but she hadn't had time to process that before the front door opened, and her mother walked in.

That had the ability to yank her out of her sleepiness like nothing else. She bolted upright, wishing she hadn't taken a nap but had spent time cleaning instead.

"This place is a mess. Where in the world am I going to put all these things that I've brought for you?" her mother said, looking around the house, somehow able to look like she was holding her nose, even though she wasn't.

She said that because she cares. She's here because she cares. She brought things for you because she cares.

Gideon's question had pierced her heart earlier, when he asked her if that was how she treated the people who cared about her.

She'd never had a whole lot of patience with her mother, because her mother was often critical and unkind. But Piper knew that was just a front. She knew her mother cared. There was no one she had ever been able to depend on more, other than maybe Richard.

"I'm sorry. You didn't say you were coming." There. That was kind. She cringed inside, because she knew she could do better.

"Of course I was going to come. What did you expect? That I would stay home when my daughter had a broken foot?" Her mother gave her head a shake, then strode into the kitchen. "I will set this on the counter. For now. What is that man doing here?" she said as she came back out of the kitchen, her eyes drilling into Gideon.

"Howdy, ma'am," Gideon said before Piper could react. "I'm Gideon. I was here last night when your daughter broke her foot.

I'm putting the addition on out back. It'll give her two more bedrooms and a bathroom, which they can sorely use."

"They certainly can. And I see you've taken off your boots before you walked into the house. I have to say, I'm impressed."

Piper blinked several times. Her mother had just told Gideon she was impressed?

She also took his proffered hand, with three of her fingers, not all five, but still, she shook it, narrowing her eyes as though gauging him while she did so.

"What did you say your name was, construction man?" her mother said.

Piper managed to not roll her eyes. It was so much like her mother to give people nicknames that felt condescending. It seemed to make her mother feel bigger, but she was actually asking for his real name, so that was a start.

"Gideon, ma'am. And did I hear you say you have more things to carry in? Can I give you a hand with them? I haven't broken anything today, and yesterday, it was just one foot."

Her mother's mouth fell open, then it closed, and then to Piper's great surprise, something that looked like it might have been a smile ghosted across her face. So quickly, Piper couldn't tell for sure, but it almost seemed like her mother's eyes were twinkling.

"You certainly can, Gideon construction person. Go on out to my car. There are seven more large paper bags that are filled with things I've brought for my daughter. I will be counting them as you come in, and I will be making sure that you do not track mud in while you do so."

"Yes, ma'am," Gideon said, and Piper wasn't sure, but it almost seemed like he was tempted to salute as he clicked his heels together, but the effect was lost since he was in his stocking feet, and then he turned around, nodding at Henry. "You want to give me a hand, young man? I think we can get these packages in without tracking in any dirt, if we put our heads together. Don't you think?"

Henry didn't look like he understood half of what Gideon said, but he nodded his head anyway, took his thumb out of his mouth, and ran back to his room hollering over his shoulder that he had to get his shoes.

Gideon gave Piper a grin, which she couldn't help but return, as he turned, waiting on Henry, and they walked outside together.

She had been sure her mother would bulldoze Gideon or make him mad, but he seemed to take her in a serious but funny way that worked.

"Who is that man?" her mother said, walking over and talking low like Gideon was still in the room.

"He's the guy who's putting the addition on the house," Piper said, feeling like she was woken up way too early and needed to go back to bed. "Thank you so much for coming. I...appreciate it."

"Looks like someone needed to come. I see cobwebs over there in the corner of the room. Don't you know how dangerous spiders are? Is it really that hard to get the cobwebs out?"

"No. It's not. I thought about them after I texted you, and I figured you'd come. You always do. And I appreciate it."

Her mom, seeming to hear the new tone in Piper's voice, the respect and appreciation, versus the automatic bristling that she usually had when her mom insulted her housekeeping skills, paused a moment and stared down at her.

"You said you broke your foot?" she asked, and her voice wasn't quite as strident as it had been.

"Yeah."

"You didn't hit your head at all?"

"Unfortunately, no. The fall did not knock any sense into me."

"How long have you known this Gideon person?" her mother said, looking out the window as Gideon walked around the house toward her car.

"He's lived in Sweet Water for a while, and I've seen him in passing at church, but yesterday was the first I'd really talked to him for any length of time."

"I think he likes you," her mom said, tapping her chin with her finger and watching as Gideon laughed with Henry as he got a bag down and put it in Henry's open arms.

"They better not drop any of that stuff," her mother said, and then she turned back around. "I can't stay. The blizzard is coming, and you know how your father is. He'll be out there insisting that he needs to shovel the walk and the driveway, and he'll blow up his pacemaker, and I'll end up driving him to the hospital in the worst blizzard this state has ever seen. Funny how people who have emergencies can get to the hospital, but the doctors can't."

Her mother sniffed, like it was a terrible thing that doctors didn't risk their lives to drive to the emergency room during a North Dakota blizzard.

But Piper didn't laugh, although the idea of her dad blowing up his pacemaker was ludicrous. First of all, that kind of thing didn't happen, and second, her dad had worked hard to get fit in the last few years since he had his first heart attack.

But her mother babied him mercilessly. Dad put up with her, because...he must love her. That was all Piper could figure out.

Maybe he'd figured out a long time ago that her mother acted the way she did because it was the way that she showed him that she cared about him.

Regardless, her mother opened the door and said, "Just set them down right here. I'll carry them into the kitchen. You go back for more."

As she was speaking, the bus pulled up to the driveway, and Lucas, Alice, and Ingrid stepped out.

"Does that child have a hole in his pants?" her mother said, glancing out the window. "Did you send him to school like that?"

Piper had just been happy that the kids had made the bus and not missed it. And they all had clothes on. She hadn't been too concerned about whether there were holes in anyone's pants.

She wasn't going to explain that to her mother though.

"I honestly can't remember, Mom. I was a little out of it this morning."

She kept her tone conversational and not defensive, the way she normally would have.

Her mom went from looking out the window to back over at the couch.

She walked slowly over and sank down beside Piper, putting her hand on her forearm.

"You've changed. There's something different about you. You're not...angry." Her mom's tone was a little softer than it had been, confident, but without the hard edges.

Piper hesitated. Any time she'd ever tried to talk to her mom about anything that was important to her, her mom had dismissed her. So she'd taken to dismissing her anytime she ever asked a question like that.

But today was different. She was honest as she said, "Earlier today, Gideon asked me if I was always unkind to the people who cared about me. It made me realize that sometimes I was mistaking people caring about me as them being mean to me. Sometimes, I feel like you're yelling at me when you tell me that my house is dirty and my kids aren't dressed properly, but just from what he said to me, it made me realize that you're not yelling at me, you're saying those things because you care, because you want your grandkids to be safe. Because you want me to do a good job. I was interpreting it all wrong. And in some ways, I was expecting you to change to suit what I thought you should be. Instead of me accepting you, and loving you, the way you are."

It was crazy how just one small statement from Gideon had opened her eyes to so much.

"Do you remember Pastor Marcel who was the pastor of our church when you were a little girl?"

"I do. I loved him." Piper wasn't sure where her mom was going with that, but the memories of Pastor Marcel made her smile. He had been a kindly and wise man, who had been able to relate to her, even as a little girl.

"He used to say that you needed to find the person who made you better and marry them."

"I think I was too much of a little girl when he was there, because I don't remember that. I wasn't listening to him with marriage in mind," she said, chuckling a little.

"I guess not. But that seemed like really wise advice to me, and I realized I had done that without meaning to. Regardless, if Gideon said that, and he's able to speak in a way that helps you see your faults, without discouraging you, if he lifts you up and makes you a better person, if he loves God and helps you to love God more too, maybe... Maybe you want to see what he thinks about children, and you in particular. He sounds like a good man."

There was a softer tone in her mom's voice, and Piper had to marvel again. What Gideon had said to her had changed her, and what she had said changed her mother. Gideon had started a positive upward spiral, just by one simple comment.

"He's a good man. For sure. But I have six kids, Mom. Six."

"I know. I told you and Richard you shouldn't be breeding like rabbits."

"Mother." Piper couldn't keep the word from slipping out of her mouth, but then she closed it, realizing that her mom again had had her best interest at heart. And if she had listened to her, she would be missing half of her children, but life would be a little easier, too.

"It's true," her mom said, sniffing the air with her nose up.

"I know. You're absolutely right. If we would've listened to you, my life would be a lot easier. Although, I wouldn't trade my children for anything. So, don't take this wrong, but while I understand and respect your opinion and part of me wishes I would have listened, most of me is one hundred percent happy that I have the children that God blessed me with, and I know God will take care of us. Those extra kids are just a little bit more of a challenge so that we can see how mighty God is."

By the time she was done, her mom was smiling and nodding her head. "You're right on both counts. You should have listened, but now this gives God a chance to work."

Piper shook her head, amazed again at how much her changed attitude had affected the relationship she had with her mother. How long had they been at odds, and it had been within Piper's ability to fix the situation, and she hadn't even known? If she had realized what a change she could make, just by changing her attitude and the tone she used when she talked to her, she would have done so a long time ago.

Or maybe she needed Gideon to challenge her. To, as her mom said, make her better.

But she didn't want her mom to have any misconceptions about Gideon.

"Mom, he really is only here to put the addition on. He happened to be around when I broke my foot, and he's been giving me a hand, but he has his own ranch, his own job, people who depend on him to help them. He can't spend the rest of his life here with me."

"No. You could spend the rest of your life with him." Her mother sounded reasonable, and Piper didn't have a retort for that.

Which was just as well since Gideon, who had not carried the other bags in because he had greeted Lucas and Alice and Ingrid as they walked up the driveway, now led the pack into the house.

Or to the doorway, since Gideon didn't come in.

"Hey, Gram," Lucas said, walking in with both of his hands around a bag, the book he'd been reading shoved under his arm, and his backpack still on his back.

"Lucas. I do believe you've grown at least two inches since last time I saw you," her mom said.

Piper smiled as Lucas's chest puffed out, and he set the bag down on the counter.

"Mom had to buy me new pants just last month, because my other ones were too short. But she said it was a good thing they were barely worn because Henry would get a lot of wear out of them."

Lucas shrugged out of his backpack and let it fall to the floor, but he kept a hold of his book.

Piper smiled, shaking her head. Lucas loved to be active, but he was also a reader. Westerns especially. If she wasn't mistaken, the book he was holding was a Louis L'Amour novel. Rather old for a nine-year-old, but Lucas had read over half of Louis's books.

Her mother walked over to Gideon and took his bag from him. "My daughter is telling me that you have inspired her to be a better person."

"Me?" Gideon said, looking dumbfounded.

Piper was tempted to roll her eyes. "Because of what you said about me being unkind to people who cared about me."

"Oh. That. Yeah, I guess I can take credit for saying it, but it takes the right kind of person to get a comment like that and have it cause them to think about how they act and then make changes. Piper's that amazing kind of person, which has nothing to do with me."

He gave her a wink, which her mother saw, before he walked back out, Lucas on his heels along with Henry.

Alice had come in, waved to Piper, and gone straight to the bedroom where Piper could hear Luna talking to herself in her crib.

Theodora was probably awake as well.

Sure enough, Luna came tumbling out after Alice a few minutes later, and Theodora was perched on her hip.

Alice was such a little mother. Piper smiled at her, talking to her sister, with Luna looking up and jabbering away, some kind of nonsense that Piper couldn't understand.

It was times like this, where things were busy, but everyone was getting along, where there were no fights and arguments, and life felt good. Even if it didn't feel rich, even if she didn't know how she was going to feed her children next week, or pay the mortgage for that matter, it still gave her such a beautiful feeling to just be alive. To feel so blessed to have so much, not in material things, but in the things that really mattered.

This was a time where she was so happy that she and Richard hadn't listened to her mother and had bred like rabbits, or whatever her mom had said.

She kind of figured that God had intended for humans to have big families. Where else could kids learn to share, to argue without being unkind? To learn to give up their way? To learn that life wasn't all about them? To learn that teamwork was so much better and life was easier when you had brothers beside you, siblings helping you, where you came home from school and had your little sisters looking at you in idol worship, so even if you had a bad day, failed a test, or got made fun of at recess, you came home and your siblings rallied around you.

Sure, life was hard, and money was tight, but her kids had that beautiful bond that only siblings shared, and her family had that happy, busy, joyful feeling that only came with a lot of siblings. She wouldn't trade it for anything.

Chapter 14

G ideon sat at the table, eating the best mashed potatoes and gravy he'd had in a long time.

Piper's mom had cooked supper, but then she left without sitting down with them, saying she needed to get home before her husband went to bed without her.

Gideon smiled at the memory of the lady. He supposed years ago she might have been called a battle-ax. But she had a soft side, which he suspected the moment he saw her, just because Piper was related to her, and anyone who was related to Piper, or had a hand in her upbringing, had to have a good side.

She hadn't been nearly as scary as what he thought she would be when he first saw her. Plus, she'd taken control of the house, the kids, the groceries, and the cleaning and cooking, so he'd gotten more done outside. The windows and doors were in, and with all the work that he had to do tomorrow and should hopefully get done the next day, they'd be ready for the storm that would come. The forecast had not gotten better. In fact, if anything, it had gotten worse.

School was still on because the snow wasn't supposed to start until late Thursday night.

"Mr. Gideon? Aren't you going to answer me?" Lucas said, from his chair at the head of the table.

Gideon sat at the foot. That's where Piper had asked him to sit, saying it was normally her seat, but she wanted him there.

She sat on the couch, her foot propped up, her plate in front of her.

He was glad she was eating, glad she had texted her clients and rescheduled, and glad they'd come to... Was it an understanding? An agreement? He wasn't sure, but the camaraderie was back between them, and whatever a person would call it, he was grateful.

"I'm sorry. I was spacing out for a little bit. Go ahead and repeat your question."

"I asked if you like to read. I'm working on reading through all of Louis L'Amour's books. This is number thirty-six," Lucas said, holding up the book he had been sitting on.

He'd done his homework. His mother had made sure of that, but from what Gideon could tell, the book had never been out of his reach.

"I'll admit, I wish I would have read more when I was a kid. I had trouble sitting still and always wanted to act out the stories rather than read them."

"I like acting them out too. But sometimes it's nice to just sit and read, and see it happen in my head."

Gideon could relate to that, and he nodded. The conversation drifted on to different books, with Alice saying that she liked westerns, too, but more along the lines of Laura Ingalls Wilder.

They both mentioned Zane Grey, which Gideon thought was a little beyond their age, but he didn't know since he had never actually read one.

Still, the kids seemed enraptured with westerns, especially historical westerns. And he couldn't blame them. He'd gone through such a stage himself, although maybe not to the extent that they had.

The kids had finished their homework, and in the hour before bedtime, they'd helped him wash the dishes, clear off the table, and wipe the counters before they went into the room to play games where they could be with Piper.

She looked better to him than she had the night before, smiling more, less like she was in pain. But he kept up with the pain pills, making her take them on the scheduled time. When she protested, he asked her to do it for him today, and then they'd talk about it tomorrow. If she wanted to take them only when it started hurting, that would be fine.

He just wanted her to have a little ease from the pain and be able to rest tonight.

It seemed to be working, as she laughed with the kids.

They played the most competitive game of Aggravation he'd ever played in his life before. A board game that was almost a contact sport, where Lucas and Alice both ganged up on Piper and him, with Ingrid ending up the winner.

Henry tried to play, but the competition was fierce, and he quit, crying in frustration.

No one eased up for him, and while Gideon was sad to see his tears, he was also happy that Henry was learning some valuable lessons.

That's what families were for. A safe place to learn that life didn't always go your way.

And it was better to handle it with a smile and a laugh than frustrated tears.

He was confident Henry would get that eventually.

It took a full hour to get Luna and Theodora to bed while Lucas, Alice, and Ingrid took turns taking showers. Then he read a story to Alice and Ingrid while Lucas got his things ready for school the next day.

They were both in bed reading books when Gideon walked over.

"Wow. You guys got to bed yourselves. That's nice," he said as he walked in.

They smiled at his praise. Henry set his picture book aside and scooted over so that Gideon could sit down beside him.

Theodora's crib was in their room as well, but she lay on her side, sucking her thumb and looking at him with big, blinking eyes.

She was used to all of the busyness and knew that bedtime was near. She didn't seem to be afraid or upset. Maybe that was because she had her brothers in with her.

Regardless, he sat down, thinking that he would read a chapter out of the book that Piper had told him that she read out of.

He was surprised when Henry said, "Mr. Gideon?"

"Yeah?"

"Would you be our dad?"

"Don't be ridiculous, Henry. No one wants to be a dad to six kids who aren't his."

"Whoa. Where did you hear that?" Gideon asked Lucas, surprised at the anger that was in his voice.

"Everybody knows it."

"I don't know it," Gideon said, although he'd said that very thing not that long ago. He tried to remember if Henry had been in the room. He was almost certain that he couldn't have heard.

"I heard the teachers talking about it in Sunday school more than once. And I heard a couple teachers talking about it in the hall at school too. How terrible it was that we didn't have a dad, but since there were six of us, there was no hope." Lucas seemed angry, and he glared at Henry for daring to bring up the subject.

"You're nice. You play games with us, and you make Mom laugh. Why wouldn't you want to stay here? We'll let you eat every day," Henry said simply.

"That's pretty much all I need, a place to eat."

"You have your own ranch. I heard that today too."

"That's true. My buddies and I have some things going on over at Sweet Briar Ranch, but it's a fun place to be. You might enjoy it there." Gideon didn't know why he said that. It wasn't like he was even thinking about being a father to these kids... Except... Maybe he was.

But he couldn't lead them on, couldn't give them hope when there was no hope.

"See? I told you. He likes us."

"And I told you to keep your big trap shut," Lucas said.

"Hey. Let's be nice," Gideon said, but his words were only half-hearted, because he was thinking.

Piper needed a husband. Miss April was trying to find her one. That had bothered Gideon all day. It had put him in such a foul mood that Baker had commented on it.

If she needed a husband, why couldn't it be him?

Lucas had his hands crossed over his chest, and while Gideon wanted to reassure him, he didn't have the words right now. He needed to have some time to think. Maybe, if he thought he could work on the addition without waking the kids up, he'd go out and just spend some time alone.

They talked for a little bit about school and books and definitely not about marriage and Piper, he read a chapter out of the book that their mom had been reading, and they all prayed together.

He turned off the light, closing the door quietly, and then he sat outside in the hall thinking for a few minutes.

Everything that Baker had said came back to him. Everything about the ladies in town wanting Piper to be married off, about looking for a widower who was twice her age, and what Lucas had insisted, that no man wanted to marry a woman with six kids.

He had to admit that wasn't exactly his dream. Trying to fit into a family where there would always be the shadow of the saintly husband over him, behind him, and around him. The idea that the kids would yell at him that if their dad was still alive, he would have done things so much better.

What if that happened? Would it matter? If the kids did hold onto the idea that their "real" dad would have been a better dad, that Gideon didn't measure up, would it matter?

After all, he wasn't working for the approval of Piper's kids, as much as he loved them, he'd be working for the approval of the Lord.

If he never became their "real" father, if Piper always looked at him and wished he were Richard...ouch. That was a hard one.

He didn't want his wife to compare him to a dead man and find him wanting. After all, when someone was gone, a person had a tendency to remember their good parts and forget the bad. He would never be able to measure up to Richard.

But again, that wasn't the point. The point was to be as much like Jesus as he could be.

If that meant asking Piper how she felt about getting married, if that meant changing his whole life plan around, if that meant being a servant to six children who needed a dad, no matter what they thought of him, and doing the exact same thing for his wife, sacrificing for her happiness, loving her without expecting anything in return, treating her like she was a child of the most high God, no matter what she did to him... Wasn't that the point?

And yet all of the questions he'd been asking himself up to just then had been about what was he going to get out of it?

Was he really that selfish? Was he really determined to live his life for his own pleasure and fulfillment?

He would never have thought he was, but he certainly had thought of himself first.

Pulling his phone out of his pocket, he pulled up Piper's number. His thumbs hesitated over the screen before they started to tap out a message.

> **Baker told me that the ladies in town were trying to find you a husband.**

> **Cassie texted me and told me the same thing.**

Her response came back almost immediately.

She was only fifteen feet away, if that, but he didn't get up. Just sat there, staring at her message. She knew it. Knew what the ladies in town were doing. He couldn't tell from the message whether she was sad or angry about it, but he would be.

> Bothered me that they'd pair you up with just anyone.

There. He sent it. That wasn't exactly everything that he felt, but it was a lot of it.

> Ha! It bothered me quite a bit too. But I have veto power, so I'm not worried about it. Is there a problem?

She probably wondered why he was talking about it. She also probably wondered why he was texting and not walking out to talk to her himself.

He couldn't really answer that, other than he just felt like he needed a little bit of quiet time to think. But he wanted to talk to her. Couldn't not talk to her, when she was right next to his thumbs, and all he had to do was hit send.

> Henry asked me to be his dad tonight.

> You are really good with the kids. I don't think they had that much fun in years. There's just something about having a man in the house, someone to laugh with and play games with. Thanks for spending time with us.

He stared at her message. That wasn't what he meant. Maybe she was deliberately misunderstanding.

> What if I said yes?

He held his breath before he hit send.

He waited. And waited some more.

Was she done talking? Had she fallen asleep? Or had he made her mad?

Most likely, she was trying to find a way to let him down easy. They had such fun banter between them, but she probably thought of him as more of a friend. Actually, she probably thought he was way too immature to make a very good dad.

Of course.

Erin came back to haunt him. The accusations she'd thrown at him, telling him that he never listened to her, that he was immature and childish, and she was embarrassed to be seen with him, and that he didn't understand her and didn't meet her needs.

When he asked what her needs were, she insisted that she'd told him over and over again, but he couldn't remember.

Maybe she'd been right. She had been right actually. He was immature.

He thought he'd grown since then though.

> **Are you saying that you told Henry you would be his dad?**

He stared at his phone. He wasn't sure what she meant by that.

> I didn't. But…I was tempted to. I didn't want to give him false hope.

He hit send, and then he figured he had to be the brave one. After all, he was the man.

So he wrote a little more.

> I wanted to, but I didn't know what you thought. And like you pointed out, you have veto power. Not just over the men that Miss April might choose for you, but over me.

He heard her phone buzz in the living room, heard the silence as she read his message. Heard more silence as she lay there, thinking about what he said, while his heart beat loud in his chest, so loud she had to hear it, and his throat squeezed tight, while his mouth was dry as dust.

"Gideon?" Her voice came out of the darkness.

He pushed to his feet and walked to where the hall opened up into the living room. He stood there, just a light from the kitchen illuminating the living room. The rest of the house was dark. And quiet.

He didn't say anything. He'd already said enough. It was her turn to say something. If she rejected him, it would be fine. Mostly fine. He'd get over it, and eventually he'd be okay watching her walk around with someone else. Watching someone else be a dad to the kids he'd started to fall in love with.

Watching someone else make a home with a woman that he'd also started to fall in love with.

"Gideon, what did you mean by that?" she asked, her voice holding wonder, but it was soft and floated in the air, like snowflakes coming down. He wanted to catch the words and hold them. Examine them before he had to answer them.

He wanted to say it in such a way that he didn't expose his heart, didn't take too many chances, didn't risk anything. Something like, you need a husband, and I'm available, and apparently your kids want me, too.

But that was the coward's way out.

"When I heard that you might marry someone else, it's hard, because I don't want to picture you with anyone other than me."

There. That was the honest-to-goodness truth, and she could take it however she wanted to. She knew their history, short as it was. She knew how long he'd known her, how long he'd been talking to her. But come on, surely she saw that he had seen her at her absolute worst. And he had to admit Piper at her worst was pretty darn beautiful.

Her trial and pain had exposed a beautiful heart, a beautiful soul, a beautiful spirit, a determined woman with perseverance who would do anything to save her children, including sacrificing her own comfort in order to do so. How could he not want a woman like that for his very own?

"I couldn't imagine marrying anyone but you."

"That doesn't mean you will."

"No. It doesn't."

"That's what I thought."

"We don't have to make a decision about that today."

"No. You have plenty of time to think about it."

"You need to think about it too."

"I've already made up my mind."

"How?"

"I've never met anyone better. Ever."

Maybe he should stay and talk. But it was late, she was tired, and he had work to do. So, he didn't say anything more but grabbed his boots and walked out the door, figuring that a few more hours of work would be just what he needed to clear his head and convince himself that the world was not going to end if she decided she didn't want him.

Chapter 15

Piper lay on the couch, blinking slowly. She wasn't sure exactly what time it was, but it was still dark. Not even a hint of dawn brightened the room.

She hadn't woken when Gideon had come back in, whatever time that was. But from the sound of his breathing, she kinda thought he was awake now.

She realized last night she had never offered him blankets or a pillow, and she totally forgot about it today, with the visit from her mom and then his startling words before he went back outside.

She wasn't quite sure where he was lying. She couldn't see any spot in the darkness, but his breathing came from over by the hall.

Before she could overthink it, she said, "Are you awake?"

"Yeah. Did I wake you?"

"I don't think so. Did you just come in?"

"About fifteen minutes ago."

"What time is it?"

"A little after two."

She digested that. He'd been out for a long time. Maybe he regretted what he'd said.

"I haven't changed my mind about anything. Just figured I'd throw that out there."

Well, that answered that question.

"Thought maybe I dreamed that," she said slowly.

"No pressure," he replied after a moment of silence.

She snorted. "Why would I feel pressure? You would be the one who would get the short end of the stick. You basically offered me a solution to all of my problems."

"But it comes with me. You don't really know me."

That was true. But it didn't have to be. "Tell me about yourself."

"I think your story is probably more interesting than mine."

"Not to me."

She tucked one hand under her cheek, closed her eyes a little, liking the rumbly sound of his voice as it carried across the darkness. A voice that made her feel secure in a way she couldn't really articulate. It's not that his voice was scary or anything like that, just...familiar on an elementary level.

"You know I was in the Air Force."

"Yeah," she prompted when he didn't say anything else.

"I don't know why I started with that. It's not really the start of my story."

"Maybe you started with what was familiar?"

"Probably with what changed my life."

"I'm sure it did."

"I was an underachiever before that. Not that the military turned me into some kind of amazing overachiever, just... I got a little more serious." He laughed. "My buddies wouldn't believe that. They think I'm the jokester, but they didn't know me before I enlisted."

"Your sense of humor is one of the things I love about you."

"It is?" he asked, sounding surprised, a different tone from the one he had been using.

"Yeah. You make me laugh. And you don't get offended over my sense of humor. I love that you assume that whatever I say was meant with the best of intentions."

"Humor can be so subjective. And I know what you mean, because I did offend people sometimes, always on accident, but I learned to be more careful."

"That's wise."

"Wise is not a word I would use to describe myself. I did any kind of stunts I could think of. We had a lake near my hometown with a huge cliff. I jumped off it more than once. Wasn't a smart thing to do, because over the years, a bunch of high school kids had jumped off it one time or another and never came back up."

That sent a chill through her. What if that had happened to him?

She said a small prayer of thanks to the Lord for watching over him. If he had died in high school, obviously, he wouldn't be here now.

"I guess God knew I needed you."

He laughed a little at that. "I don't know. I'm hardly the hero type. Like I said, I just wanted the attention. I guess... I guess my parents were too busy and didn't spend much time with me. When they did, I felt like they were always trying to mold me into someone I didn't want to be. I fought against it by goofing off. I was voted class clown. It was a pretty obvious decision. Since I'd do anything to get a laugh."

"The person you're describing isn't the person that you are now."

"No, I know. I just... If we ever go back, that reputation is still there in my hometown."

"Where was that?"

"You don't think I'm native North Dakota?"

"I know you're not." She spoke with confidence. Because while she hadn't lived in Sweet Water all her life, she had lived in North Dakota.

"How do you know that?"

"It's the way you look. After you spend so many winters in North Dakota, you get a survivor's look about you. You don't have that. You just have that twinkle in your eye that says you still think life is fun, and you're out to have a good time."

"That's sad."

"I'm just teasing you. Mostly."

He didn't say anything for a while, and then he said, "You have a survivor's look about you. But I wasn't attributing it to the North Dakota winter. I was attributing it to all the trials God has given you, and I was asking myself, why? Why have you gone through so much, and I really haven't gone through much of anything. Nothing that God gave me. All of my trials were mostly my own fault. Stupid decisions that I've made, and consequences for my dumb decisions."

"Maybe the Lord didn't have to give you trials, because you found your own." She laughed a little, snuggling down deeper in the couch. She wasn't afraid of anything that he was saying. It was obvious to her that he had learned from the things that he'd been through. He'd become a better man because of them.

"I'm trying to scare you off, and you keep complimenting me."

"If you've changed your mind, say so. But telling me about your past isn't going to make me afraid."

"I was engaged once."

Her heart dipped. All right. That changed things a little for her. She didn't like the idea that there was a skeleton in his closet. One that he cared for so much he had asked to marry it.

"What happened?" she asked, feeling compassion as well as fear.

She was probably beautiful. Anyone who would catch Gideon's eye would have to be. And smart. Way too smart to ever get married rather than go to college and end up with six children and no husband. Successful. All the things that Piper wasn't.

"She was a good woman. Ambitious. She wanted to be successful in life. She didn't want to settle for average, or slightly below average, which is where I typically was."

He blew out a breath, almost as though he was frustrated with himself. And Piper wondered if that was because he still considered her the one that got away. Maybe he longed to go back and do things differently.

"She said I was too immature. I think my humor amused her at first. It was different than what she was used to. But the more time she spent with me, the more I annoyed her. And finally, she just couldn't imagine spending the rest of her life with someone like me. She told me I was immature, never paid attention to her, didn't treat her the way she should be treated, and didn't listen to her. Some of these accusations I didn't even really understand. Finally, she threw my ring back at me and walked out."

"Ouch."

"At the time, it hurt, but looking back, we would have been miserable with each other. She was way too seriously ambitious for me. I guess I still don't really care about status or about having the biggest and best and newest of anything. I guess... I guess I like what you have here. A family that laughs together, warm companionship. A fun type of busyness, despite the fact that the kids fight sometimes. And it's a lot of work."

"You've got that right. It is a lot of work." She moved her leg, pain shooting up from her foot as she did so, and the warmth that she felt seemed to dissipate as she searched for a comfortable spot.

"I guess I've never been afraid of hard work. I did a lot of goofing off, I told you that, but some of my pranks involved a lot of preparation, and it didn't matter how elaborate they were, I was willing to put the work into getting the laugh. I suppose, that really translates into me being willing to put the work in to have the reward of a big, happy family."

"You were born to be a dad. It's a shame that you're not."

"Honestly, if Erin and I had gotten married and had children, I'd be a single dad right now, or a weekend dad, or whatever they are when you split the kids because she would have wanted them, just because it would look better. It's hard for me to imagine her being a really great mom. She was...too concerned about climbing ladders to be held back for long by motherhood. But she would have done her duty."

"Sometimes that's what it takes. I have to admit, there are times where I've stayed when I really wanted to leave, and it was all out of a sense of duty. Feelings come and go. Sometimes they are more go than come." She was just being honest. That was the total truth. There had been more than one time when she thought that life would be so much easier if she just walked out. She didn't have money to support her kids anyway, and they'd probably be better off as wards of the state.

"I don't believe that."

"It's true. I guess I shouldn't be talking to you about it. Maybe I shouldn't even admit it. You might change your mind about me. But I haven't always stayed because I love my children and they're little cherubs who are perfect and never do anything wrong and I've never gotten frustrated and angry with them. Even the deep bonds of motherhood sometimes feel like they are frayed to the breaking point."

"You're still here."

"Yeah. Because of duty. Because it's the right thing. Because I know that if I left, no matter how badly I might want to be out from underneath the burdens that I'm carrying, I would regret it. At the end of my life, I know I cannot look back on it and be proud of what I'd done and accomplished if I did it because I walked out on my kids. I just couldn't."

"I don't think anyone expects life to be peaches and roses all the time. Sometimes you feel like quitting. It's the times when you feel like quitting, when you stick it out, that show your character."

"Maybe. I guess I don't feel like I have any kind of great character, it's just... I don't know. Maybe a lack of opportunity. Where would I go anyway?" she said, laughing a little, because that was true. She wouldn't know where she'd go even if she did decide to walk out.

"I don't believe that. There are plenty of places you can go. At the very least, you can start walking down the road with your thumb out."

"Right. Like jumping out of the frying pan and into the fire."

"Sure. But sometimes you're so desperate to be out of the frying pan that the fire actually looks like a good spot to be."

"And so you get up close and personal in it, and then you'd do anything to go back."

"You can never go back."

"That's true. Things change. You can try, but once I walk out on my kids, even if I tried to come back, it's not like they would ever forget that."

"Absolutely. You can't erase things from their mind. As much as it might be nice to at times."

"Oh, I agree with that. Even erasing the little things. Like the meltdowns I've had, or the times I yelled at them when I was frustrated or angry. You can't take it back, so you look at what you've done, and you try to think how you can avoid doing that again. Because I don't want my kids to grow up and be so relieved to be out of my house. Or to have memories of their mom screaming at them. Or to think, God forbid, that their mom doesn't love them, or want them, or thinks that they're a burden."

"You have to be deliberate about your parenting. Or it just happens. And you get what you get." He sounded thoughtful, like he was thinking about it and maybe had been before they started talking.

"Yeah. Maybe it helps that I think the way I do, because I like to look at the end, decide how I want things to end, and then move forward with that goal in mind." She huffed out a breath, a little laugh, at her seriousness. "Of course, you're just setting yourself up to be frustrated, because life never turns out the way you want it to. And the only person that you can even partially control is yourself. And honestly, I'm not even that good at controlling me. I certainly can't control the decisions the people around me make, or how my clients all behave, who lives or dies, or anything, really."

"That's all true, but you're onto something. I have a tendency to think the opposite way. I don't think about the end, I think about the details of the day. I suppose we get to the same place, just in different ways. But I see it as taking care of things in the right way as they crop up. Not allowing them to snowball to bigger things. I suppose, if I hadn't been such a goof-off in school, I would have been a perfectionist. That's a little bit scary."

"Yeah, the word perfectionist definitely doesn't belong with six children. You'd go crazy."

"I'll keep that in mind. I assume you don't want to be married to a crazy person."

There. He did it. He said the married word.

"Do you think about Erin much?" she asked, totally changing the subject.

He was quiet for a bit. That scared her. She didn't want to be married to someone who was still crushing on someone else. Longing for someone else. Or thinking in his head that Erin was the perfect person for him and anyone else would be him settling.

"No. I haven't thought of her in years. Not until yesterday, and then it's funny, being around you made me think of her. Probably not in the way you're thinking, because I thought of how wrong she was for me. Of how serious she was, and how she never got my sense of humor. Of how she considered me immature and was always trying to make me grow up. Of how she looked at me and saw someone who needed a lot of changes, versus you. Maybe I'm wrong, but I feel like you look at me like you like who I am. That you see me, seeing the best in me, and see my mistakes as mistakes and not things that you need to change in me. Not like I'm a child that needs to be disciplined in order to grow up to be the kind of man you want. I feel like...you think I'm already that man."

"You are. I love that you're so good with the kids, like you're a kid at heart, but not immature. That your desire is to raise them to do right, and you are not afraid to correct them, but you don't correct them for things that are just childish things, but for character issues. I...think you seem to have a natural way about you."

He laughed a little, almost a self-deprecating laugh. "I guess it's totally natural for a woman who has six kids to admire any ability I have to relate to children."

She got the feeling that he wanted to be admired for being a man, not just for being good with her kids. That he wanted her to see him in a romantic sense.

Could that be true? It didn't really seem like something a man would long for, but she wasn't sure.

"That's just one thing," she finally said. "I..." She was a little scared. Scared to tell him that for her, it wouldn't be hard to fall in love with him. "I told you I love your sense of humor. I love how you make me laugh. I feel...entertained, but also like I entertain you. Like you enjoy being with me. Almost as much as I enjoy being with you. I so often feel like I'm a mom. And that's all I am, but with you... I feel funny and pretty, like there's more to me than just my ability to take care of people."

"There's so much more to you," he said, fervently, like he couldn't believe she would ever doubt it.

"When all you do all day long is mediate fights and change diapers and put curlers in people's hair, or cut it just so, you start to think that your worth is in serving people, and I know that that's a Christian way to think, but I guess I want or maybe just long for more. For romance. Is that sacrilegious?"

"I think God put that desire in you. I don't think that's a wrong desire. After all, God talks about how He romances the church the way a man romances his bride. So, He acknowledges that there's a time and a place for romance."

She heard his smile in the darkness.

"I don't know if you've ever read it, I think it's in Deuteronomy, but I could be wrong, how a man was supposed to not go to war for a year after he married, so he could console his bride. I think the word is console. I often wondered about that. I mean, I guess she's leaving her parents and living with someone she barely knew, since marriages then were probably mostly arranged, unless I'm mistaken. "

"I think you're right."

"So, I'm not sure about that console word, but I wondered at times if that meant that the man had a year to help his bride fall in love with him. To bind her to him and develop the feelings of affection that they didn't have a chance to develop before their marriage."

"Interesting." She had to laugh. "I guess I would have read that and assumed that the man had a year to get his wife pregnant, because they had to procreate before he went to war."

They laughed a little together, and he said, "You might be right about that, but maybe that's the Bible's way of saying that the man isn't supposed to force his wife, but spend time allowing her to get to know him before they move on to the procreation."

"I think that's a really good idea," Piper had to say, thinking that if they got married, maybe that was the way Gideon would be thinking for them as well.

"Yeah. I think men and women are a little different, but God knows."

They were quiet for a bit. That was as intimate as their conversation had gotten, and it made Piper a little uncomfortable. As far as she could tell, they hadn't agreed to get married, and that conversation topic skirted the edges of her comfort zone.

Finally, his voice broke the stillness. "I don't want to push you, but my offer is still there."

"Your offer of kissing me?"

"Well, that one for sure, but if you want to marry me, I'd like that."

She shouldn't have teased him about the kissing. But maybe that was part of the romance she wanted. Talking in the dark was a good start, hearing about his childhood growing up was another one, but she didn't want to be just someone he talked to, someone he admired. She wanted...a little more.

"I accept both offers," she said, surprised at the words as they came out of her mouth.

She couldn't hear any movement across the room, not even breathing, and then the rustle of clothes indicated he was moving.

Still, it was a bit of a surprise when she felt his presence beside the couch.

He bent down beside her. "Both offers?"

"Yes," she breathed, her hands clutching the edge of the blanket and the toes of her good foot flexing. What was she doing? Was she crazy?

"So... Are we looking at a certain time?" His head leaned down so that his breath fanned over her face. She couldn't see him in the dark, nothing but the outline of his head, as he bent over her.

"As soon as possible, I guess. We probably can't do it before the storm."

"The kissing we can definitely get done before the storm. Not that I'm looking to check that off my list. I figure that'll be something I want to work on for quite a while."

She laughed. It sounded a little nervous.

"The marriage... We could probably do it today if you want." He sighed. "Except you can't go anywhere to get a license."

"It's possible that someone would come to me. I happen to know the clerk who works in the courthouse."

"Ah. A woman with connections. I like it."

It reminded her a little bit of Erin, and she didn't smile the way she might have.

"What?" he asked, like he could feel her deflate even just a tiny bit.

"Erin has connections. I...still wonder if maybe you'd be better off with someone like her."

"No. Erin was with a lawyer the last I heard. I know she's much happier with him than she ever would be with me. And like I told you, I couldn't see us staying together. Not just because of her. Although, I hope once I say vows, I stick to them. Just... God worked it out so I didn't marry the wrong woman. She was wrong." His hand touched her cheek, his fingers trailing down. "You're not."

She tried to swallow, but her throat was dry, and she found it hard to breathe.

His fingers were soft and gentle, and she closed her eyes.

When was the last time someone touched her without wanting something from her? Wanting food, wanting clothes, wanting her comfort?

She didn't mind giving, and giving and giving some more, but his touch wasn't trying to take from her, his touch was giving to her.

It was a nice switch, and she didn't try to think, to talk, to say anything or do anything other than close her eyes and enjoy it.

"Piper?"

"Hmm?" she murmured.

"I told you last night I want to kiss you, and you told me just now we didn't have to wait, and I was wondering if now is a good time?"

Now was probably a terrible time. They were alone in the living room, and it was the middle of the night. If she were talking to her daughter, she would advise against ever kissing a man in the middle of the night when they were alone together. Unless they were married, of course. But that was just her wanting to give advice that would make it as easy as possible for her daughter to stay pure before her marriage.

An outdated idea that even Christians scoffed at anymore, but one God felt strongly about. He had harsh words for fornicators and adulterers. And kissing was just putting one foot on a very slippery slope. A slope that led directly to fornication if a person wasn't very, very careful. Why would she play with fire?

Still, she figured she was safe enough with her broken foot in such a precarious position, and Gideon wouldn't do anything that might hurt her.

She was sure.

And...had he really suggested they get married in the morning?

"I'd really like that," she said softly.

He made a noise, it sounded like a half laugh, half groan, as his lips touched her temple. "This is crazy."

"This?"

"Me. The way I feel about you. How it feels so right to be next to you. How I want to be closer. How the idea of kissing you is all I've thought about since the words came out of my lips, and even before that. How I wanted to come to bed a whole hen of a lot earlier but couldn't stop thinking about this."

His words sent shivers up her spine and made her smile. It was what she wanted. To know that he didn't look at her and just see a mom of six kids, but found her appealing. That he loved her character, loved her sense of humor, but there was more.

It spoke to her feminine vanity, she supposed, and it gave her the bravery she needed to unclench her hand from her covers and put it around his neck, her fingers touching the soft hairs at the back, feeling him shiver and let out another small sound.

"You make it hard for a girl to get any sleep," she said, not knowing how else to tell him that was all she had thought about before she'd fallen asleep, only to dream about him.

"I think that's a compliment." There was a bit of smile in his voice, but there was a deep rumble there as well. "I almost don't care." His lips brushed her jaw, and his knuckles touched her cheek.

Her thumb skimmed along his stubble, loving the way it poked at her skin and felt smooth at the same time.

"We barely know each other. Am I crazy?"

His finger stopped and it was like he held his breath before answering. "I don't think so, but I'm probably not the best person to ask about that right now, since I'm feeling a little nuts myself."

She turned her head, brushing her lips against the rough edge of his jaw. He moved his head, his lips finding hers and she sighed against them, her head whirling and her body humming with excitement and passion, but there was a feeling of contentment, of rightness, that whispered deep in her soul as his lips settled more firmly over hers.

She was so lost in his kiss, it took her a second after his head lifted to realize that Theodora had woken up and was crying.

"What should I do about her?"

Gideon's voice was a little rough and his lips brushed her cheek as he spoke.

"She might go back to sleep if we give her a few minutes."

He let out a shaky breath. "I'll have to thank her later. I'd pretty much forgotten my name and was only thinking about getting closer to you. Her crying barely registered."

"I didn't even hear it." Her words were a little shaky.

He laughed softly, pressing his lips to her forehead. "I think I might go outside and work a little more. I'm not going to go to sleep anytime soon."

"That hardly seems fair. I'm not going to go to sleep, either, but I'm stuck here."

"I think I like having you where I know exactly where you are." His hands cupped her face and he kissed her nose. "Sounds like she's settled back down."

"I thought she would." She hadn't gotten to the point where she was grateful for the interruption. She wouldn't have minded kissing for a lot longer, although he was probably right. It was a good thing they stopped.

"I'll see you in the morning," he whispered as he pressed another soft kiss on her forehead and stood up, pausing before he walked away.

She felt bereft and had to press her lips together to keep from asking him to come back. He was trying to do the right thing and she wanted to help him, not make it harder. Of course, his character and desire to do right was more appealing than a million passionate kisses.

She was afraid she was falling hard for her unintended knight in slightly tarnished armor.

Chapter 16

Tuesday morning after they got the kids on the bus, the clinic called with a cancellation, so Miss Brooklyn and Miss Cassie came out to watch the kids while Gideon took Piper in to get her foot set and casted.

Gideon had to admit he appreciated Piper's calmness as she gave loose instructions for the kids but told the ladies to just do whatever worked for them, and as long as no one died, and she preferred no ER visits, everything would be fine.

He supposed there wasn't anything wrong with giving pages of instructions, but he liked the more laid-back, the kids will adjust to whatever you do approach.

Piper had protested a bit when he had gone to carry her off the couch and down the steps.

"I have crutches. I can do it."

"It hurts you when you jiggle your foot, which is almost impossible not to do on the crutches. There's no point in starting out the day in a lot of pain."

They hadn't had much time to talk, actually none, since the kids got up early, and from the time the kids got up until they got on the bus, there was no peace.

Then immediately after the bus had left, Cassie and Brooklyn had showed up, and it wasn't until he got Piper settled in the truck and he walked around and got in the other side that they were finally alone.

He supposed that was the way life was going to be. If they actually went through with what they talked about last night.

He had every intention of going through with it, but he had a nagging feeling that Piper was going to back out. He wasn't sure why. Maybe it was just old insecurities rearing their head. The idea that he was too immature, that Erin had told him he wasn't good enough. That he did not make her feel loved and cared for. That he didn't pay attention to her. Whatever she said.

He noticed that Billy still stood in their yard. He'd never heard of him visiting anyone's house outside of Sweet Water.

But, as far as he knew, he had been at Piper's house for two days.

Piper had said something about squirt guns that showed up at the same time as the steer. So strange. But Gideon had to admit that there was something altogether different about Billy. After all, the whole town swore he was a matchmaking steer, which didn't make any sense, no more sense than the fact that the entire town also swore that he was in love with the pig.

He supposed every town had its eccentricities.

"I'm sorry about last night," Piper said before they were even out of the driveway.

Yeah, that's what he had figured.

He stared at his hands on the steering wheel before lifting his eyes back to the road. What was he going to say? Did he fight for her? Did he just let her go?

Didn't someone say that love was letting go?

Wasn't love fighting to keep someone, too?

"It wasn't your fault," he finally said, since that was the truth, and he didn't know what else to say.

"No, but that's what happens when you're with me. I have six kids. There aren't going to be too many times when we're going to have total peace and quiet." She smiled a little. He could see it out of the corner of his eye, and it gave his heart lift. "Like now."

She wasn't saying what he thought she was going to.

"So..." He drew the word out. "You're not apologizing about last night because you're sorry that it happened, you're apologizing because you're sorry we got interrupted?" He tried not to let any hope enter his voice. Even though it was burgeoning in his chest like a flower in the sun.

"Yes. What did you think? That... I regretted it?" She sounded incredulous.

"I'm sorry. You sound like you can't believe that, but in my experience, that's what seems to happen to me."

"That people regret being with you?" She still didn't seem like she understood.

"I told you, Erin said I was too immature. She changed her mind about me. I guess, I guess maybe there's a part of me that is just waiting for you to do the same."

"Gideon. I have six children. If anyone's going to be changing their mind, it's going to be you." She said that firmly, like that was just the commonsense way to think.

He rolled it over in his head. He supposed that was what the rest of the world would agree to. That he was the one who was a little crazy and who should definitely rethink things before he made a firm decision.

But that wasn't the way he felt. He felt like he was being given the honor of being with Piper. Being a father to her children. He knew her children were the most precious things in the world to her, and she was trusting him with them.

"Piper?"

"What?" she asked, sounding a little impatient, despite the calm and patient tone of his voice.

He shook his head. Putting his turn signal on, he pulled off to the side of the road.

He put the truck in neutral and shoved the parking brake down before he turned in the seat, putting his arm over the back and hooking his other hand over the gearshift as he stared at her.

"I understand what you're saying. I understand that you probably are going off the things that have happened to you, the same as I am. Where a man looks at a woman who has a bunch of kids and doesn't want to be shackled to her. I get it. So I'm not saying you're crazy, I guess... I guess I just want you to understand that's not the way I'm looking at it."

Her eyes were big, and they blinked slowly as she listened, absorbing what he said.

"I know how precious your kids are to you. I know what an honor it is for me to have you say that I can come into your life and into your house and be a husband and a father to you and your family. That's a privilege you are giving to me. It's not something I'm stooping to. It's a precious gift. I don't want you to think of it as anything less, and I don't want you to think that I think of it as anything less. Because I don't. And children aside, you are a beautiful and capable woman, someone I admire more every minute I spend with you. Someone I can't stop thinking about. Someone I want to be with. More than anything. I've... I've never felt this way before, where I want to protect you and hold you and care for you and spend every waking second with you, and every sleeping second too, but what I am doing is beyond my feelings, beyond how I feel. It's something that I know God has worked out in my life. Worked out that I'm putting the addition on your house, this happened with your foot, and things are just falling into place. I don't have any doubt about being with you, getting married to you, and while I find it a little bit scary—"

He wouldn't admit that to just anyone. Maybe he shouldn't be admitting it now, but he had to be honest.

"—scary because I have so many people looking at me, not just depending on me to provide and care for them, but looking at me as their example, someone they want to emulate. I... I'm not nearly good enough to have six children wanting to be like me. But I know God can grow me into the man I need to be. I know it, and even though I think it's going to be a little bit painful, I'm excited about it too. I'm excited that the Lord wants me to be in such a prestigious position. Not prestigious in the eyes of the world, prestigious in the eye of eternity. Do you understand?"

He finally ended, seeing her eyes fill with tears.

"Piper?" Panic rose in his chest. "I didn't mean to make you cry. Actually, I was kind of hoping that would do the opposite." He couldn't keep the panic from coming out in his voice a little. What had he done that had caused her to be so upset she needed to cry?

"That was beautiful," she said, though her throat was obviously too tight, and she could barely talk.

"You're crying." He pointed out the obvious.

"Happy tears. Grateful tears. Tears because...too many emotions and no way to express them." She shrugged an apology and lifted a hand to wipe her cheek.

He leaned forward, using his thumb to wipe the tears from her other one, carefully and gently. Treating her the way he felt about her, that she was precious.

After all, that's the way she had treated him. Like he was good enough to entrust him with her children and herself. That was one of the biggest gifts she could give him, one of the highest compliments she could pay, and he wasn't going to take it for granted or act like it didn't mean anything.

"I don't know how you managed to turn this so completely around," she said, shaking her head and bringing her hand up to hold his fingers next to her cheek. She laughed softly. "Anyone who looks at us will see you doing something really kind, something that most men wouldn't do, knowing that I have nothing to offer, and you act like I'm giving you the biggest gift in the world by allowing you to be here, and it's actually the other way around, but you just made it seem like it's not. You make it seem like you value, not just me, but also my children, our family, and that being a part of it is precious."

"That's because it is."

She was still shaking her head, smiling, but disagreeing. "You're right. But no one ever sees that. No one ever says that. It's so out of—"

"Just because popular culture doesn't value children and large families doesn't mean that I don't. Doesn't mean that I don't see."

"It's just amazing. It's unbelievable that I found what feels like the one person in the entire country who would look at me and my children and see us as a privilege and not a pain."

"I guess that's just the way the Lord works sometimes. He brings those people together who were meant to be."

Her eyes lifted to meet his, and there was gratitude in them for sure, but something else. Something that looked a lot like...love. "There have been times in my life where I've wondered what in the world God was doing to me. Why he was putting me through so much hard stuff, and then He goes and gives me such a huge gift, and I don't even have words to say how amazing and awesome He is."

"And I'm the huge gift?" he asked, a smile tilting his lips up.

"Yes. Even if I didn't have six children, I would wonder what in the world someone like you, someone so capable and strong and confident and funny and hardworking, would see in someone like me."

"You make me sound a lot better than what I actually am," he said, still smiling. She made him feel pretty good too. That she would think that he was all that. They grinned at each other for a few minutes, and then he said, "After we're done at the doctor's, do you want to go get a license?"

"I'll call the pastor right now."

"We can plan on this afternoon."

"Before the kids get home from school?"

"Whatever we can fit in."

"All right. Whatever works, works."

"God seems to be orchestrating this in His time anyway, so we might as well let our wedding day follow His time as well."

"I like that. It's the best way to do it anyway."

Chapter 17

Lucas thumped out of the classroom toward the cafeteria.

He was still upset with Henry for saying something to Mr. Gideon.

If they had allowed Mr. Gideon and his mom to spend time together, they might have figured out that they liked each other. But when a man was pushed into something he didn't want, he had a tendency to fight.

Lucas knew that much from reading his westerns.

Men balked when they were forced to do something.

But he really couldn't fault Henry. Back when he was four, he didn't know any better either.

Still, a person had to be a little more subtle when they were trying to work people to get what they wanted.

Not that Lucas thought that was a great idea, but when it came to his mom getting a husband, he would do whatever it took.

Especially if they would get a dad as good as what Mr. Gideon would be. He actually played games with them last night.

He knew from talking to his friends that most of their dads were too tired when they were done with work to do anything with their kids.

A couple of them played baseball on the weekends, and one or two of them worked in the garage with the boys beside them.

Lucas had been jealous of the boys who still had dads, and he didn't understand why God took his.

As he was walking down the hall, he saw a group of girls talking quietly, and he slowed down a little, recognizing Merritt and Sorrell, along with their friend Toni. Toni and Sorrell were his age, and they were in his class. But he usually didn't talk to them.

Toni was tall, almost as tall as he was, and he really liked her, but when he chased her at recess, she told him to go find someone else, because she didn't play little games like that.

He wasn't sure exactly what that meant, but he figured that it meant she didn't like him at the very least.

They stood beside the water fountain, and Lucas was going to keep walking, but something Sorrell said caught his attention.

"It worked fine with my mom and her new husband. It'll work for you, too. We just have to figure out what man we need to get to eat it."

"We need to give it up. My mom said if I just pray, God will bring me a dad."

Lucas stopped. He'd been praying for a dad for two years, and God hadn't done anything for him.

But Sorrell had a point, because she did get a dad. Maybe God was just slow sometimes.

Or maybe God didn't think they needed one. That seemed to be what Toni's mom was saying.

"Are you guys trying to get a dad too?" he said when he stopped, half expecting them to ignore him.

"We got one. We did it with the Marry Me Chicken."

"I'm not sure if it was the Marry Me Chicken, or if it was Billy. I think Billy had a lot to do with it," Merritt said, and Lucas reevaluated his opinion of her. She might be a baby, since she was only eight years old instead of nine, but she was giving credence to the rumor that went around Sweet Water, that Billy the steer was a matchmaking steer.

"Billy's been out at my house for the last week."

"Maybe he's trying to match your mom with someone!" Merritt said excitedly. "What has he been doing?" she asked, like the steer was sitting in their living room on a dating site putting a profile up for his mom or something.

"Nothing. He's just standing in our yard."

"Just standing there? Isn't he doing anything?"

"He really can't do anything other than eat. It's not like he has hands."

"No, but there has to be some reason why he's out there. He has to be doing *something*."

"No. Nothing. Unless you count the squirt guns that showed up about the same time he did. Mom told us it was too cold to play with them, but she let us do it a couple nights right before we took baths."

"Squirt guns?"

"Yeah. We found four of them about the same time he showed up."

"Interesting," Merritt said, pinching the bridge of her nose together and scrunching her eyes down like she was thinking really hard.

He didn't see what there was to think about. Cow, squirt guns, and...nothing else. That was it.

"Aren't you always reading westerns?"

This question was from Toni, and he paid attention.

"I do. I've read a lot of Louis L'Amour and some Zane Gray. Do you like westerns?" he asked, trying not to sound too eager, tempering his tone so he sounded chill. Or at least a little bit chill.

"No, but haven't you ever read about a shotgun wedding?"

He frowned. "That's like where the angry father forces some dude to marry a woman that he's compromised. That he kissed and shouldn't have?"

"Exactly," Toni said, nodding her head and crossing her arms over her chest like she just made a great point.

Unfortunately, Lucas had no idea what great point she just made.

"He doesn't see it, Toni," Sorrell said, lifting her brows at Toni, like she was going to have to explain more.

He wanted to thank Sorrell for noticing, since Toni had seemed a little clueless about the fact that he wasn't following her, not even a little bit.

"That's why Billy brought the squirt guns."

"How do cows carry squirt guns?" he asked, and again he felt like he totally missed the point when Toni rolled her eyes.

"Don't worry about the how," Sorrell said. "You have squirt guns. Use them."

"In what way?"

"You know adults hate to get wet. They're like cats. They'll do anything to avoid being squirted."

"Especially in the house. They hate being squirted in the house and having water inside."

"All right. So I see myself getting in trouble if I try to squirt my mom in the house. I don't understand what that has to do with anything."

"It has to do with this. You use the squirt guns to hold your mom and Mr. Gideon captive until they agree to get married. Actually," Sorrell had a gleam in her eye, "It would be really great if you could have the preacher out there when you do it."

"How am I getting the preacher out to my house?" Lucas asked, feeling like he was about seven steps behind the girls and their thoughts. He didn't understand anything they were saying, like they were speaking in a different language.

"Your mom just fell and broke her foot. The preacher should be visiting anytime. That's what preachers do."

Actually, he just read a book not that long ago where there was a shotgun wedding, and that's what it had taken, a preacher, plus a man and woman to get married. But they had had real guns.

"Do you think the squirt guns will work?"

"It's worth a try, isn't it? Do you have a better idea?" Merritt crossed her arms over her chest and tapped her toe, like he needed to get with the program.

"No. I don't." Unfortunately.

He didn't even have a glimmer of a better idea. Nothing.

"Not everything that you try will work. But you won't know whether it will work unless you try," Toni said, sounding a little less stuck up than she had earlier. It reminded him of why he liked her so much. Aside from the fact that she was tall.

"All right. I'll see if I can do that. I'll try at least. I'm not sure how to get the preacher out, but..."

"Don't worry about it. I'll text Miss Cassie. She's a softy and one of my mom's best friends. I'll get her to get my mom to go out with her to visit your mom, and I'll suggest that she might need a preacher, just because your mom probably wants to pray a lot, since breaking her foot hurts and people like to pray when they're hurt."

Lucas nodded, thinking that sounded a lot more complicated than anything he would have come up with, but figuring it might work. Although, he didn't really know Miss Cassie, and while he knew Miss Jane from the diner, he would never have the nerve to text her and ask her to come to his house, even if he had a phone, which he didn't.

He wanted to stay and talk with the girls, but he couldn't think of anything else to say, so he mumbled a thank you and walked off.

That afternoon on the bus ride home, he talked with Alice and Ingrid about his plan.

Their concern was that Henry wouldn't be able to keep from squirting people and would ruin everything. They didn't want to include him.

But even though he was little, and even though he messed everything up last night by asking Mr. Gideon to be their dad, Lucas wanted to include him because he was the only brother he had, and he wanted them to be best friends.

That's the way it was in all the westerns that he read. A man could always count on his brother.

So, when they got off the bus and saw two cars sitting in the driveway, with Henry playing outside in the small sandbox they had, Lucas insisted he needed to be part of it.

Maybe he'd mess things up again, and this was pretty important, because he didn't want to lose their only opportunity to get the best dad they'd ever be able to find, but at the same time, he wanted Henry to feel included. Because he knew what it was like to not get to be with everyone else.

Usually they walked up the driveway, but today all three of them ran, and they stopped at the sandbox and told Henry their plan.

Lucas couldn't help but notice that Billy the steer was still standing over by their shed, right beside where they put the squirt guns.

Chapter 18

Piper sat propped up on the couch, the bemused smile that seemed to be on her face all day still tilting her lips up and making everything that went on around her feel like a dream.

Of course, the throbbing in her foot made everything all too real.

The doctor had casted her foot and told her she could use crutches but that she was to stay off it and keep it propped up as much as possible.

She and Gideon had talked just a little on the way home about whether or not she should start working again. They hadn't made a decision.

Everything was busy in Rockerton, with everyone expecting the impending storm. North Dakotans were used to bad weather, but this was supposed to be bad even for North Dakota.

Still, the courthouse was open. They got their license. They set up a time for the pastor and managed to get a hold of Miss Helen and Miss April, who were coming out to be witnesses.

The kids were fine when they got home, although Cassie and Brooklyn didn't stay long, having to get back to work themselves. Piper knew what a sacrifice it was to come watch someone's children, and she appreciated her friends making time and leaving them with two casseroles. One for supper and one for the next day. What a blessing her friends were.

She appreciated them watching the kids and making things easier, as well.

Not that she typically did what was easier, but considering how much they had to get finished and with the storm coming, it worked out better to not take them. Plus, it gave Gideon and her some much-needed time to talk. She was so glad he had stopped the pickup and told her what he had earlier. She wasn't having doubts, not really, but there was some anxiety, and she'd wondered if she was doing the right thing.

With his speech, all those concerns disappeared, and she knew beyond a shadow of a doubt that there would never be another man who would be more perfect for her or her children. And as much as she liked Gideon, she wouldn't have married him if he hadn't wanted her kids.

When she became a mom, her life had to stop being about herself, had to be about doing what was best for her children.

They'd eaten in town, having a quick meal at the diner, before they got back to the house. She'd barely gotten settled on the couch when the pastor knocked on the door.

"It's a busy day, anyway," Gideon said with a grin as he walked to the door to open it.

She hated that she was unable to do much of anything. But she appreciated the fact that Gideon wanted her to follow the doctor's orders exactly, and he was willing to take care of her to make sure that she did.

It would be so much harder if he was insisting that the doctor didn't know what he was talking about and wanted her to continue with her normal routine.

She probably would have done it, and it would have been to her detriment.

She was so blessed to have a man who truly cared.

"Come on in, Pastor. We appreciate you being able to do this at the last minute."

"It's part of my job, and it's always a pleasure to marry two people who want the Lord's will," the pastor said as he walked in. He shrugged out of his coat as he stood by the door. "It hasn't started snowing yet, but apparently we're supposed to get a good bit more than normal. I should have offered to bring something out with me. I hope you guys didn't need anything?"

"We were in town earlier to get the license, so we grabbed a few more groceries while we were there, and I think we're set," Gideon said as he took the pastor's coat.

"I thought you said that Miss April and Miss Helen were coming as witnesses?"

"Yes, actually I think they just pulled in."

"That's great. I wanted to do a little marriage counseling before the wedding, so hopefully that's not an issue," the pastor said with his brows raised.

Gideon look surprised, and Piper groaned a little in her soul. She didn't want this to take forever. She wanted to get married and be done with it.

But she supposed she'd take all the help she could get to have a good marriage. She felt like Richard and she had done okay, but Gideon was a lot different than Richard, and he intimidated her just a little, because she felt like she wasn't really worthy of him.

It helped that he seemed to feel the same about her. Still, her relationship with Gideon was going to be much different than her relationship with Richard. That was one thing she was sure about.

"If you don't mind, we'll do it over here by the couch. Piper is supposed to keep her foot propped up as much as possible, and so far, she's been a good girl," Gideon said with a wink at her.

She wanted to stick her tongue out, unlike something a good girl would do, but she just wrinkled her nose at him and then smiled at the pastor. "I'm sorry I didn't get up to greet you."

"No. That's fine. I heard about your foot just today and had planned on coming out anyway. A wedding is a much better reason to come out to visit someone than a broken foot though."

"I have to agree about that," Piper said as the pastor settled in a recliner, his Bible and another small book along with a few notes sitting in his lap.

Miss April and Miss Helen came in, taking their coats off and getting settled, then Gideon sat down on the floor next to Piper's head.

It was silly, but it made her feel special that he chose to sit on the floor next to her, rather than in a more comfortable chair. It made her feel like he really wanted to be with her, and she put her hand on his shoulder. He put his hand up and wrapped his fingers around hers, his feeling warm and rough and somehow infusing her with strength and happiness.

She didn't know how he did it, but every time she touched him, it made her feel better. Despite the fact that she hadn't realized it was possible to feel better. She would have said she felt just fine.

"All right, we're gathered here today to perform one of the most sacred ceremonies a Christian can witness, a sacred and timeless covenant, one God instituted for man."

The pastor smiled, looking around at each of the people sitting there. Then he turned his focus to Gideon and Piper.

"I mentioned to Piper that I wanted to do a little bit of marriage counseling before I conducted the ceremony. I usually have couples come in to meet with me at least four times a month or so before I perform the marriage. However, there seems to have been a rash of quick marriages here in Sweet Water, and I've gotten some condensed marriage counseling in, despite the fact that's not probably the most ideal way. Sometimes we need a little bit of time to digest information and think about things."

He smiled at Piper, and she nodded. It was absolutely true that sometimes she needed to think about things.

"However, I'm fairly certain that the two of you will continue to read and study and do your best to have the best marriage you can. Because of Piper's six children, it is extremely important that the two of you strive to have a great relationship. That will affect your children for decades to come. Probably for the rest of their lives. Of course, children can learn from bad examples, but it's far easier to emulate good ones."

Gideon nodded, and she realized he'd never really said what his childhood had been like. She'd just learned about Erin, and that had thrown her for enough of a loop that she hadn't thought to ask about anything else.

"I want to look at a passage today that is not typically used in marriage ceremonies. But it's one that, if you apply it to your marriage, there is no possible way that your marriage could fail." He grinned a little. "Have I salted the oats?"

Gideon's hand squeezed hers as she smiled at the pastor. She was certainly interested in hearing about something that would make her marriage fail proof.

"I want to read you a verse from Mark chapter 9 verse 41. 'For whosoever shall give you a cup of water to drink in my name, because ye belong to Christ, verily I say unto you, he shall not lose his reward.'"

The pastor looked up from his Bible. "This passage isn't exactly talking about being kind to people, it's about talking about other people being kind to the disciples of Christ."

He eyed both Piper and Gideon. "Both of you are disciples of Christ. That's what Christian means, little Christ. And while this passage is specifically talking about people other than disciples being kind to actual disciples, you could apply it to one disciple being kind to another. That's how I will use it today."

The pastor looked down at his notes, as though thinking about how he wanted to start, and then he raised his head again.

"Everything that you do, every single thing that you do to your spouse, is being done to a child of the most high God. I think, when we get married, and especially after we've been married for years, decades even, we forget that. We get used to people. It happens in friendships as well. We take advantage of our friends, of our family, our parents, siblings, and, again, spouses. But those people, if they're Christians, are all children of the Almighty God. Now, I don't know about you, but I feel pretty protective of my kids. I don't like it when people aren't nice to them. I want to do something to get back at anyone who would dare to do something to my children, I want to do something even worse in return. I'm going to protect my kids. I'm going to keep them from being treated badly. I'm going to keep them from being hurt. I'm going to notice when someone hurts my children, and if I can't do something to fix it, I'm going to keep that in mind. Now, as a Christian, God calls me to forgive and forget, and He says He's the righteous judge."

The pastor let that sink in for just a minute, and then he said, "How much more is the righteous judge going to watch you be unkind to your spouse, and be upset that you're treating His child that way? Just because you're married to him doesn't give you any special rights to be unkind. In fact, marriage is supposed to mean the opposite. You're supposed to be even more kind to the person you vowed to spend the rest of your life with, vowed to love and to cherish, to protect and to serve." He smiled. "Let's just park on that word 'serve' for a while. Isn't that what a cup of cold water is? You give your spouse a cup of cold water, you're serving them, and in this passage, God promises that he will make sure that the person who gives his disciple a cup of cold water will not lose his reward."

The pastor shifted. "Is that what we're working for? Heavenly rewards, not earthly ones? So, you have the opportunity, every day, day by day, to put rewards in heaven. God promises that you won't lose them, and God always keeps His promises. So, the more difficult your spouse is to live with, the more opportunity you have to lay up treasure in heaven. Where moth and rust don't corrupt, where thieves don't break through and steal. This is the surest retirement plan you can possibly have. Where God is keeping your treasure. And you can build it with your spouse."

Across the room, Miss Helen shifted in her chair.

Piper didn't look at her. Maybe she was just uncomfortable, although she was sitting in a recliner.

Piper herself wanted to wiggle. After all, she had six children, and they were all opportunities for her to build treasure in heaven as the pastor said. Because on a daily basis, she provided cups of cold water to them. Along with food, clothing, stories, smiles, and love. All of those things were building treasure in heaven. And the more she did, the harder her kids were to handle, the more treasure she had.

She certainly had never thought about it that way. But a mother was uniquely positioned to have more treasure in heaven than anyone else in any other job on earth.

Interesting that God would bless a woman, a stay-at-home mother, in that way. He must think very highly of that position.

The pastor continued. "The Bible also says in Matthew 25 verse 40, 'the King shall answer and say unto them, Verily I say unto you, inasmuch as ye have done it unto one of the least of these my brethren, ye have done it unto me.' In this verse, we also learned that doing something kind for someone is like doing it for Jesus. You look at your spouse, and you see Jesus. You serve him like he's Jesus. You do things for her, like she's Jesus. You treat her like she's Jesus. Anything you do, you can do like you're doing it for Jesus."

The pastor cleared his throat.

"It's easy to think about but very hard to implement. Because when someone is unkind to us, or even not unkind, just uncaring, what do we want to do? We want to treat them the same way, don't we?" He smiled like he knew exactly how that was and had done it a few times himself.

Piper appreciated that he wasn't preaching at them, he was talking to them, as someone who had been in their places and had done the same exact same things.

"There is no reward in that. That's easy. That's what everyone wants to do. If someone is nasty, an unsaved person is going to be nasty back. Christians are called to be different. We're called to a higher standard of living. And that would be doubly so if your spouse isn't saved, which doesn't apply here but does apply in some marriages. After all, if your spouse is unsaved, and you act toward them the same way they act toward you, you're no different than they are. Not that I'm saying that Christians are better, but we're called to a higher way of living. We're supposed to be different because we know Jesus." He paused. "Are we?"

That was a powerful question. Powerful because Piper knew that so many times, she wasn't any different. She wanted to be, though.

But wanting to be didn't mean anything if she didn't make herself be. If she didn't take the steps to actually be different.

"Just two verses in the Bible, one talking about acts of kindness and you won't lose your reward, and the second talking about acts of kindness and everyone that you do them for is like you're doing it for Jesus. Those two verses, if you put them first and foremost in your marriage, both of you, will guarantee that there is no way that your marriage could fail. After all, you wouldn't want to cheat on Jesus, would you? So therefore, you're not going to look at another man or another woman, because if you do that to your spouse, it's like you're doing it to Jesus. Also, keep in mind that your spouse is a child of God. If you cheat on them, you're cheating on the Almighty's little girl. I wouldn't want to have to stand before God and explain that one. Maybe you're braver than I am," the pastor said with a smile, and Piper appreciated the bit of levity.

After all, it was a little fearsome to think that she was going to pledge her life to someone and then answer to God for how she lived that life, how she treated that person, not to mention, she was already answering to the Lord for how she treated her kids.

So many times, she just focused on the love and happiness portions of the Bible. She didn't focus on the portions that were hard or scary or forced her to examine her life and make changes that were uncomfortable or difficult or that caused her to give up what she wanted, give up her way, and made her understand that her life wasn't about herself.

"The Bible says in two different places for we shall all stand before the judgment seat of Christ. In Romans 14, and again in Second Corinthians 5." The pastor mentioned those verses without checking his Bible.

It was probably good to have those places memorized. It would be a good reminder.

"The Bible says all. All of us. In Second Corinthians, it says that 'every one may receive the things done in his body, according to that he hath done, whether it be good or bad.'"

The pastor sighed a little.

"It's always nice to focus on how much God loves us and cares for us and all the things He's going to do for us, but we forget that we were bought with a price. That that price was more than we could ever pay. And because of that, because of that great debt we owe, we should be driven to serve the Lord in whatever way we can. Even if it's just a little bit of kindness we show our spouse day in and day out. God rewards that. And you will stand before the judgment seat of Christ and give account for what you've done. For me, I don't want that to be the most uncomfortable thing that I've ever had happen. I want God to look at me and say 'well done, thou good and faithful servant.' I'm sure that's what you want too. A marriage, a Christian marriage, is the perfect place for you to learn and grow and practice. Practice giving of yourself, practice kindness, practice giving cups of cold water."

The Pastor closed his Bible and opened up the smaller book.

"This will be an odd wedding, since I usually have the couple stand. I know the doctor requested you stay off your foot, so we're going to have this wedding sitting down. I believe, if I'm not mistaken, this will be the first wedding ceremony I ever conducted like this."

Chapter 19

Helen shifted in her chair.

The pastor's little message to Piper and Gideon had hit her square between the eyes. She had needed it. And badly. She had been treating her husband the way he treated her. With an unconcern for him while going over in her head all the little things he did that showed he didn't care about her.

She'd been keeping track of all his faults and had been gloriously overlooking all of her own. She hadn't been giving cups of cold water to her husband in any way.

She couldn't push that out of her head, even as she watched them get ready for the ceremony. She'd been doing the right things, cooking his meals, washing his laundry, cleaning his house, but she hadn't been doing anything extra. All the times she could have been kinder had gone to waste as she sat and felt sorry for herself because he didn't measure up to the ideal in her head.

"Mom!" a voice called as the door burst open.

Helen turned, and her eyes widened.

Four of Piper's children walked in, holding squirt guns.

Helen blinked. Squirt guns?

"Lucas?" Piper said in a voice that mothers everywhere used, a voice that asked him simultaneously what he was doing and why he was doing it because he knew better. It also held a warning, that he better quit.

But the boy held his ground.

"Mom, Alice, Ingrid, and Henry and me all have something to say."

"You do?" Piper asked, humor lacing her tone, and Helen tried to hide a smile. Piper had something to say to them too; it was her understanding that the kids didn't know that Piper and Gideon had planned to get married. Maybe they should have, because Helen was betting that was going to come as quite a shock to the children.

But then, her mouth almost dropped open at Lucas's next words.

"We decided," the boy started, nodding at his two sisters who held their squirt guns pointed out, dripping on the floor, "that Mr. Gideon better marry you. You guys were alone last night in this house, and you're not married. You always told us that people who aren't married aren't to live together. So we're here to make sure that Mr. Gideon does right by you."

It had been years since Helen had to bite back a giggle, but she found herself coughing to cover the sound that she couldn't keep from erupting from her throat.

First of all, the kid sounded ridiculous, like he'd read one too many westerns, and second, he had no idea that he had just interrupted his mother's wedding.

"You're right, Lucas. I was here last night, and I'm not married to your mom. So, I think you're right. I probably should make an honest woman out of her. Isn't that the way it goes?" Gideon said calmly, although he did eye the squirt gun, not wanting to get wet any more than any of the other adults in the room wanted to.

Lucas had his mouth open like he was ready to argue, but his shoulders drooped, and it's almost like his entire body deflated. Not necessarily in a bad way, just in a way like he had not been expecting that turn of events.

"Really?" he asked, in a far less strident tone.

"Really. You're right. I'll marry her," Gideon said, then he looked at Piper. "If she'll have me. She's a pretty amazing woman, and she might want someone a little better than I am."

"No!" Alice spoke for the first time. "We want you. You play games with us, and you read stories, and you're pretty good at putting additions on, although you haven't finished yet, so we're not entirely sure about that, and you need to learn how to cook better, but it's okay, because Mom can teach you. She's a good cook when she has time."

"You didn't like my macaroni and cheese?" Gideon asked, like that was the only important thing that she had said.

"It was gluey," she said, shrugging her shoulders while Ingrid nodded beside her, and Lucas nudged Ingrid with his shoulder, pointing to her gun, which had dropped to the floor.

"Hold it up. It's not going to do you any good if you can't use it if you need it."

"You told us we weren't to squirt any of the adults because it would make them mad."

"They're not supposed to know that," Lucas said, through gritted teeth, although the entire room could hear him clearly.

Helen glanced back over at Piper to see what she was making of this.

Her kids were being a bit disrespectful, but they were doing it for a good cause, and Helen hoped that Piper was not going to discipline them. Not for the guns in the house, and not for the fact that they were going to demand that Gideon marry her.

Piper just looked like she adored her children though, and she said, "So you really want Gideon to marry me?"

"Mom. He'd really make us a good dad. Don't you want us to have a father?"

"Don't you miss the father you have?" she asked, with a glance at Gideon.

He looked stoic, but he lifted his chin, as though he understood that was a legitimate question. Maybe he would have preferred to hear the answer in a room with not quite so many people in it, but sometimes life didn't work out so that things happened in the best way they possibly could.

"I do. I miss him, but he's not here, and he's not coming back. And you work too hard. You need someone to help take care of you. Plus, we need a dad."

"Maybe we could have talked about this before you felt the need to come into the house with your guns drawn," Piper said in a very reasonable tone.

"I'm sorry. I didn't think of it myself, I was talking to some friends at school, and I was reading a couple of my westerns, and they told me that I ought not to just sit around and complain about how things are, but I ought to get up and do something about it. Something about being the change I wanted to see in the world or something."

Helen tried not to snort.

"I see. Well, squirt guns might not be the best way to be the change you want to see in the world, but I suppose they will work today." She turned to Gideon. "I suppose, if you don't want to get wet, you might have to marry me today."

"It's kind of convenient that we have the preacher here."

"Indeed."

"And I happened to bring my sacred sacraments book, which has the wedding vows in it," the pastor said, obviously going along with what Gideon and Piper had started.

Which made Helen wonder if the kids would ever find out that it hadn't been their idea for the two of them to get married. Maybe Piper and Gideon would let the children think that their determination to do something about their situation had caused them to create a family.

Aside from the fact that squirt guns were not the answer to the world's problems, Helen thought it was probably a good lesson for the kids to learn that if you wanted to see a change, you probably shouldn't sit around and complain, but ought to get up and do something. Instead of expecting other people to do things for you.

Which went back to what she had been thinking about with her own husband. She had been expecting him to be the husband that he was supposed to be, and she wanted the change in their marriage to come from him. It hadn't occurred to her until just today that maybe she should step up and do a little more, even though it felt like she was already doing the most.

If she believed the Bible, and she did, God promised a reward for her. No matter how little her husband responded, she would be rewarded by God for everything that she did. That in itself should be enough for her to work tirelessly, no matter what the people around her did.

She watched as the children filed the rest of the way in, still holding the squirt guns, and shut the door behind them. They stood on either end of the couch, guns raised, looking seriously at the preacher as he cleared his throat and began.

Helen wished she had a picture. She'd never seen anything so cute. The kids instigating a shotgun wedding, or a squirt gun wedding, she supposed would be the more accurate, although less popular, description.

As she listened to the vows, she thought about how they might talk about how their parents got together because of them. She thought it was probably a good idea to let the kids think that they had a hand in it, since they were much more likely to accept Gideon as part of their family if they thought they had perpetrated the wedding.

"Do you take this woman to be your lawfully wedded wife? To have and to hold from this day forward, for better or for worse, in sickness and in health, for richer, for poorer, as long as you both shall live?"

In light of what the pastor had just said a little earlier, those questions she had heard a hundred times in a hundred different weddings took on a new meaning.

She had made those promises long ago. And she felt her husband hadn't lived up to his vows, so she'd been lax in keeping hers. Oh, she hadn't cheated, but she hadn't truly meant that she was going to continue to be the best wife she could be when he wasn't the best husband he could be. She based her actions on his.

Which wasn't biblical in any way. After all, she was called to be like Christ, who certainly did not base his actions on anyone else's but came to die for everyone, despite their sin. The Bible said while we were yet sinners, Christ loved us. And yet, she wanted her husband to not be a sinner, to earn her love.

She hadn't even articulated that, and yet that was what she had been doing.

Weddings always made her feel bittersweet. As she looked at Gideon, gazing into the eyes of his bride, he smiled at her, and maybe his hands trembled a little, but there was an eagerness in his gaze, a heat there that was unmistakable to Helen, and yet so much tenderness, so much of his actions showing that he would cherish his wife, that his desire to protect her and provide for her was real, almost palpable. And his affection for the children who stood at the head and foot of the couch was obvious as well.

Piper looked up at Gideon like she adored him, the way Helen had looked at Edgar on their wedding day. What had happened to them? Years of trouble and trial had maybe hardened them some, but she had allowed her feelings and actions to slide. She needed to work on getting them back.

She thought of that as she drove home after dropping Miss April off at her house.

The plan came into her head as she fixed supper, and she found herself fixing her husband's favorite, chicken pot pie.

She'd just put it in the oven when he came home from work.

His job as a construction crew boss was demanding, and he'd mentioned multiple times that he was getting too old for that line of work.

He was on his feet a good bit of the day and sometimes had to work away and didn't make it home.

"How was your day, honey?" she asked as he came in.

He looked up in surprise. Normally she greeted him, but she tacked on the endearment, as well as made sure her tone was soft.

He noticed the difference immediately.

"Fine," he said before looking back down to take his boots off. "Call me when supper's ready," he said, padding to the living room.

Well, that made all of her good intentions want to crumble into the dirt.

But he worked for her, he had been true to her, as far as she knew, and he wasn't unkind. He just didn't expect kindness from her. Maybe he was the same, just feeling like it was too much effort, and didn't really think about putting that into his marriage anymore.

Of course, if he was kind to her, she would probably return the sentiment. Or she could be kind to him, and he would be brusque like he was just then.

Still, she dried her hands off on a tea towel and stood in the middle of the kitchen, her hands folded across her chest, before she grabbed a cold soda out of the refrigerator and walked into the living room.

"I thought you might be thirsty," she said, offering him the soda as he sat with his feet propped up in the recliner, TV remote one hand, his eyes fixed on the screen.

"Thanks," he said, reaching for it and glancing at her, before his eyes were back to the wall behind her.

"The chicken pot pie will take thirty minutes to bake. I thought I would rub your feet while I'm waiting for it to cook."

She could tell the second he stopped seeing what was on the screen, although his eyes didn't move. Then, they kind of narrowed as they went back to her.

"You want to rub my feet?"

"Aren't they sore?" she asked reasonably, settling herself down on the floor in front of him and reaching up to pull down one of his socks.

"I guess if you're gonna rub them, I'm not going to turn that down."

"I didn't think you would," she said, smiling a little at him, even though he was looking at her with suspicion.

She was thankful that her husband was one of those few, blessed people whose feet did not stink, although she would rub them anyway, even if they did.

She finished pulling his socks down and did what she hadn't done for years.

She had been doing it for several minutes while he scrolled through TV stations, but he hadn't turned the volume up, and so it was quiet in the living room.

Finally, he said, "Do you remember when you used to do this all the time?" His voice was low and a little contemplative. It wasn't like Edgar to be sentimental, but it almost sounded that way.

"I remember. I don't know why I quit."

"I don't either. I always loved it."

"I used to miss you so much when you were gone, and I was so happy when you came home. It was like a reward for me to be able to do something to thank you for working all day for me."

"Is that what it was?"

"I loved you too. I wanted to show it."

"Past tense?" he asked, and maybe that was the elephant in the room neither one of them ever talked about.

"No."

He didn't say anything to that, and neither did she.

Finally, he said, "One of the guys on the crew that I supervise quit without notice today. There are so many open jobs in this economy. It doesn't even really go against a guy anymore to not give notice. If I was going to get the job done that we needed to get finished in order for the electrical crew to come in and get their job started tomorrow, I had to do his job. So, I ended up doing both today. It was a hard day."

"You never could stand to not meet a deadline." He hated not getting his work done. He liked to be ahead, and while he pushed his crew, whatever crew he supervised was known as the best. He took pride in that. Sometimes she resented it, because he put more effort into his job and doing a good job than he put into being a good husband. It bothered her.

"You always understood that. A lot of guys' wives didn't."

She hadn't had a choice, but she didn't say that. Instead she said, "I'm sure they'll come around eventually."

"Most of the time, they just get divorced. Because the wife doesn't understand the pressures of the job and how hard a man is pushed to do his best all day long."

"It's stressful."

"It is. Then they come home to a wife who nags and fusses at them."

She had been guilty of that over the years. But he didn't mention it. And she supposed she appreciated that.

"I suppose the wife would only be doing that because she's jealous."

"Jealous?"

"Jealous of his job."

Edgar sat with his eyes fixed on the wall, but she didn't think he was actually seeing it. "So they're jealous that he's putting so much time and attention into his job...instead of them?"

It's funny how much easier it was to talk about when they weren't talking about their own relationship, but talking about *other* wives being jealous. Other wives nagging. Other men putting too much time and energy into their job.

She supposed that it felt less like an attack, more like a conversation when it wasn't personal.

"Yes. That's exactly right. I suppose, women take to nagging and complaining because it's just a natural thing to do. But I don't think nagging or complaining ever really works to change anyone. Not in a positive way, anyway."

"I agree with that," Edgar said, like the idea of someone nagging was just the worst thing that could ever happen to him.

Helen looked down at his foot, continuing to massage the bottom, careful not to have too much of a light touch around his toes, which had always made him ticklish and didn't feel good.

She ran her fingers up his ankle. It was funny, but his ankles got just as tired as his feet did, and he always liked that.

"I guess I can see that. Men put such stock into doing their job. Mostly because they get yelled at by their bosses if they don't, but it's also a prestige thing."

"For sure. They want the recognition of having the best, doing the best, being the best, but there isn't nearly the prestige or recognition for being a good husband."

"No. Although... I suppose bosses come and go, but wives don't."

"They shouldn't anyway," Helen said easily.

"Maybe that's the problem. You kind of feel like you've conquered that area of your life, and with your job, you haven't. There's never a point where you're in a position that you can't be replaced."

"And eventually you will be."

"That's right." He didn't say anything for a moment, and then he said slowly, "But the wife is still there."

"She is."

They didn't say anything more, and Helen wasn't sure whether anything changed or not, but as she pulled the sock off his other foot and started to massage, she felt like maybe it didn't really matter. It would be nice if he worked on his marriage as much as he worked on being good at his job, but she supposed it would be worse if he worked on being good in some kind of hobby instead. At least when he worked at being good at his job, she benefited monetarily. And she supposed, if she cared about it, she also had the prestige of having a husband who was good at what he did.

If he spent all of his spare time becoming a good golfer or doing something equally fun for him, it would be worse.

Still, she supposed whatever it was, what the pastor had said today applied across the board. Doing kind things for her husband as though her husband were Jesus, as though she truly believed what the Bible said, and that she would be rewarded for her good works, doing things because she loved God and wanted to please Him, was more important than making sure that she got treated the way she was supposed to be treated or that other people treated her just as well as she thought they should.

At her age, she wouldn't have thought that she could have learned something so basic, or she supposed it wasn't so much that she learned it, as much as she'd been reminded of it.

She had needed the reminder.

Chapter 20

Their company had left, and Gideon stood in the kitchen, washing dishes.

Billy the steer hadn't quit bawling, and as the sound reverberated around the house once more, he looked over to the couch where Piper lay.

"Did you say there was some hay in the shed?" he asked.

They had stopped at the feed store and grabbed some feed for Billy, but the hay they'd ordered hadn't been delivered. They had said because of the storm, it might not be, and they'd been right.

"There is. I... I'd kind of like to go out because there's a couple of things that I'll need to move, and I want to be careful with them."

"You don't trust me?" he asked, grinning at her and knowing it wasn't a matter of her trusting him, just a matter of her wanting to know where things got put.

"Of course I trust you." She knew he was just teasing her. She also knew that he knew that she trusted him. After all, she had just agreed to marry him, had married him, today.

"Let me finish this last dish, and then I'll come over and carry you. We'll all go out. I could feel the temperature dropping when I opened the door to let the pastor and the ladies out. After all that nice weather, I think we might be getting the snow they're calling for."

"Hardly. It's been so beautiful the last two days."

"Maybe that's Billy's problem. He can feel the mercury dropping and knows that we're getting a storm."

"That could be."

The kids played around them, with Lucas and Alice and Ingrid keeping a rather low profile.

He figured that they were still concerned that they might be in trouble for the stunt they pulled.

He and Piper would be laughing for a really long time over letting the kids think that they had pulled off the wedding.

Someday, they'd probably ask about a license, and that might be when the truth came out.

Piper and he wouldn't lie, and he figured they would talk about it later.

Still, the whole idea made him smile every time he thought about it.

In just a few moments, he had the rest of the dishes done, and he scooped up Piper while Lucas carried Luna and Alice held Theodora on one hip.

It was a family excursion out to the shed as Ingrid and Henry skipped around them.

"My goodness, the shed door's open. I don't know who would leave it open like that."

"Looks like there's some fresh dirt moved around, like something's been walking in and out." He didn't recall seeing that yesterday, but he might not have been paying attention. He and Baker had been pretty focused on working on the addition.

"Maybe Billy has been making himself at home in the shed after all."

Ingrid, who had been put in charge of the flashlight, shone it inside the shed as she looked in the cracked door.

"I think there might be animals in there," Ingrid said, wrinkling her nose and looking back at the adults behind her.

Immediately, Gideon wished he wouldn't have brought everyone out. If there were some kind of animals that would attack when they got cornered, or something with rabies, he didn't have hands to protect everyone while carrying Piper.

Maybe it was just something that was searching for a warm place to ride out the storm.

"What kind of animals?" Piper asked, and he could hear the same concern in her voice.

"I think they might be pigs," Ingrid said hesitantly, like she couldn't quite figure out why she was saying what she was saying.

"Pigs?" Piper and Gideon said at the same time. While Theodora squealed, because Luna was squealing most likely, Lucas and Alice also expressed their disbelief.

"I think so," Ingrid said, shrugging and looking back in the crack.

"Go ahead and push the door open a little wider," Gideon said. "Slowly," he added hastily, just in case it was something that he was going to have to deal with.

"I don't want to drop you," he said under his breath.

"I don't want to be dropped," Piper said, right back to him, making him smile.

He knew she'd understand if he had to set her down in a hurry to try to protect someone, although...pigs?

"Are there wild pigs in North Dakota?" he asked, as stories he'd read of feral pigs attacking and killing people came to mind. Particularly a sow who was defending her babies.

"I don't think so."

"Stand back," he said to Ingrid as she pushed the door open.

She stepped back so that she was right in front of him. Which was probably the worst place she could be if he needed to move quickly, but...he didn't think he needed to.

"Is that the pig from Sweet Water?" he asked, and the thing that really gave it away was the fact that she had a green ribbon around her neck.

"I think it might be," Piper said, squinting. "Shine the light right on her," she commanded Ingrid.

Ingrid complied, not moving from her position with her back against Gideon's knees.

Billy, who had been standing at the corner of the shed, moved over, and the side of his horn pressed against Gideon's hip.

It was like he, too, was looking in the shed.

"Do you think this was what Billy was bawling about?" Piper asked as she saw the steer beside her, then looked back in the shed at the pig who most definitely had babies swarming around her.

"It could be. They say in town that he's in love with her. Although, I'm pretty sure he's not the father," Gideon couldn't help but add.

He was glad he did because Piper giggled.

"I'm going to set you down right here on the lawnmower seat. Is that okay?"

"Please do. You can't do anything while you're holding me, and I know I'm getting heavy."

"I was most definitely enjoying holding you, so that's doing something, and I don't really want to set you down, but I think... I think Munchy just had her babies in our shed," he said, still not quite able to believe that was what happened.

"When did she show up? I never saw a pig?"

"First Billy came. Then we found the squirt guns. And now we have baby piglets in our shed. I wonder what's going to come tomorrow?" Lucas said eagerly.

"Four feet of snow?" Piper said, answering his rhetorical question.

"Besides that. We get snow all the time."

"Four feet of snow will pretty much cover your head," Piper said. "We don't get that much snow all the time."

"Do you really think it would be taller than me?" Lucas asked, clearly excited. Like he hadn't talked about it for the last week with his classmates, teachers, every adult that he'd seen.

"That's what they're saying," Gideon said, carefully setting Piper down and walking back over to look at the pig. "I don't think we should get too close to her. I've heard that pigs can be rather protective of their babies, and while she isn't a huge sow, she can still bite."

"I want to pet them," Ingrid said, inching closer.

"Ingrid. Mr. Gideon told you to stand back, and you need to obey."

"Yes, ma'am."

Henry stood beside Ingrid while Lucas and Alice stood side by side, each of them with a child still in their arms.

"They're so cute!" Alice said, obviously wanting to move forward just as Ingrid had.

"They are pretty adorable, but... I'm not sure what to do with them."

"We got Billy feed, but we didn't get anything to feed a pig."

"That's exactly what I was thinking." He looked around behind him. "The snow hasn't started yet. I suppose I could run back into town and grab something for the pig. After all, if we get as much snow as they're calling for, none of us are going to be going anywhere for a while."

"That's true."

"Is there anything else we need in town?"

"No. I think we're pretty well stocked up. I... I wonder if we should tell the town? Who owns her?" she asked, knowing that from what she'd heard, no one really claimed it. It was just the town's pig.

"I don't know. I guess maybe they adopted us."

"Or they were trying to make a match," Piper said, suggestion in her voice and irony heavy in her tone.

"Well, that worked." Gideon turned around, smiling at her.

"Didn't it?" They laughed together.

Neither one of them had set too much store on the idea Billy was a matchmaking steer, but there they were, the steer at their house, and somehow they ended up together. Married. And the idea that the steer was in love with the pig was rather ludicrous, except he was the one who bawled and brought them out to the shed in time for them to be able to go get Munchy food.

If that wasn't love... It might not be romantic love, but it was a love that took care of his friend.

The kids watched the pigs for just a little bit more before they all filed out of the shed, shutting the door, and petted Billy on the head.

"Thanks for letting us know, bud."

Billy looked just like a steer normally did, contentedly chewing his cud, his eyes placid, his stance calm and relaxed. He didn't look proud of his accomplishments or like he cared one way or the other whether people got married or didn't.

But... Gideon just couldn't say for sure that steer didn't have something to do with the fact that he was here, married, and thinking Piper was the absolute best woman in the world.

Chapter 21

"**L** ook! It's snowing!"

All six of the kids ran to the window where Ingrid pointed to the soft flakes of snow that floated gently down past the floodlight outside.

Henry and Alice had been helping Gideon make the Chex mix, while Ingrid and Lucas had been following Piper's directions on how to put up the old tent she'd stored in the back of a closet up in the living room.

Piper had confessed to Gideon that the tent leaked, and she'd been meaning to throw it away, but the kids had been excited about staying up late and sleeping in the living room together. They'd figured the electricity was going to go out, so he'd made a fire in the pellet stove and they'd been working on making Chex mix.

He met Piper's eyes across the room. She sat on the floor with her back against the couch, her casted leg stretched out in front of her. She was smiling.

"It's hard to believe after the winter we've had that they could be this excited about getting more snow." He shook his head. He was certainly ready for the winter to be over and for spring temps to be here to stay.

"This time of year, we know it won't last long," Piper said, somehow knowing he was ready for spring. Or maybe she was feeling the same as him.

He scraped the last of the Chex mix in the bowl, picked them both up and carried them into the room. The kids were still gathered around the window, looking up at the dark sky like they'd be able to see anything other than the dark underbellies of lowering clouds.

He still couldn't quite believe the way things had worked out. Or that he was married.

Married.

His wife watched him, her eyes soft. He couldn't believe she'd trusted him enough to pledge her life to him. To trust him with her children. It was a privilege he didn't have words for, but the responsibility also weighed on him, to have all those people looking to him to provide and protect, to nurture and raise.

But, behind that weight of responsibility was the absolute assurance that Piper and her kids were absolutely what God wanted for him.

"I have the kids' bowl here." He held up the bowl in his left hand. "And the adults' bowl here."

"You made two batches?" she asked, her brows lifting.

"Yep. You guys were so into putting the tent up, you didn't even notice."

"No, I didn't." She huffed out a laugh. "I honestly wasn't even sure we were going to get the tent up. It didn't look good there for a while."

"I had confidence in you." He put the bowls on the coffee table and settled himself down beside his wife.

"So, are they the same?" she asked, bending forward and peeking into the bowls.

"We have two kinds, Mom!" Henry came racing over, crashing into Piper, eliciting a grunt from her.

"Careful, kiddo. Your mom still has a hurt foot."

"Oh. Sorry, Mom." He looked contrite immediately. Gideon could totally relate to him. It seemed like yesterday when he had more energy than he knew what to do with.

JESSIE GUSSMAN

"It's okay. You didn't bump it at all. Now, tell me about the Chex mix."

"One is spicy hot. Mr. Gideon said that you and he would eat that one and the other is for us kids."

"Spicy hot?" She lifted her brows and looked at him. He grinned, putting his arm around her shoulders and loving the feel of her against him.

"You don't like spice?"

"I don't like being in pain while I eat."

"Then you'll want to eat the kids' bowl, which, works out perfectly, because I'll have the adult bowl all to myself. First time in my life I was actually the adult in the room."

"Hmm." Piper gave him a look. One that teased as well as promised.

"Ingrid and Luna both like spicy things." Henry spoke, not realizing that he was deflating Gideon's dream of having the entire bowl of Chex mix to himself.

"They do?" he asked, trying not to sound as disappointed as he felt.

"Yep." Henry said, settling in beside his mother.

Theodora toddled over, climbing up on Gideon's lap and settling down like she belonged there.

"I can't believe how she's taken to you," Piper murmured.

"Kids love me," he said, smirking, although it was the truth.

"Moms do, too," she said, ignoring his arrogance and giving him that soft smile that made his heart feel warm and melty.

He bent over, kissing her temple, breathing in her scent and loving the feel of his family around him, his wife beside him and the snugness of the impending storm making everything feel cozy and perfect.

"Will Billy and Munchie and the babies be okay?" Alice asked, coming over more slowly, chewing on her bottom lip.

"I'll be checking on them. I'll have to shovel the snow away from the door and maybe even the roof, periodically, if we get as much as they're calling for."

"Can I help?" Lucas asked eagerly.

"I was hoping you would," Gideon answered easily.

His shoulders straightened and he lifted his head, a pleased, proud look on his face.

Gideon's gaze went from the boy to Piper, who looked at him like he was her hero. He didn't deserve that look, but that didn't mean he wasn't going to enjoy it.

He lowered his head, kissing the corner of her mouth softly.

"I love you," she whispered.

"I love you more," he whispered back.

"I don't think that's possible."

"I have a few decades to prove it. You'll see."

"Game on."

The kids were chatting about the tent and the Chex mix and their excitement about staying up and the steer and the piglets, but Gideon wasn't really paying attention. He moved his lips from the corner of Piper's mouth to her temple and wondered what the years would bring. Obviously, there would be hard times. But Piper was the kind of woman who would stand beside him through them all. He honestly couldn't wait.

Chapter 22

Travis fingered the diploma that he still held in his hand. His mother hadn't made it to his graduation. She'd promised she would come, but it had been scheduled for Monday night, which she had taken off, but then her latest boyfriend had told her that he wanted to go out, and she ditched Travis in order to go out with him.

She'd known the dude for three weeks. They were still in the infatuated with each other and neither one of them could do any wrong stage.

Travis figured it was pretty bad that his mother had had so many boyfriends he knew they went through stages.

Regardless, he'd seen Ellen in the audience. Tadgh and Ashley had been beside her.

Tadgh had been so much like a father to him the last almost ten years. It meant a lot that he had come out on the best night of Travis's life so far.

Even better than the night he'd won the football game for his team.

He walked offstage after they'd switched their tassels and thrown their hats, careful not to lose his diploma. He'd worked hard for it.

He'd gotten up by himself, gotten himself off to school, along with his getting his brothers up, and there had been so many days when it would have been easier to not. His mother wouldn't care, but he wanted to set a good example for his brothers, even though he often thought about quitting. Not necessarily because he hated school, but because he wanted to have a full-time job so he could work on getting custody of his brothers. His mother hadn't been much of a mother.

That pretty much had been a pipe dream, though. Teenagers didn't get custody of their little brothers, especially when his mom was still around.

He really didn't want to get the state involved, either, because most likely they would be taken from her and put in foster care while the state did an investigation. It could be years, but it would definitely be months, before he would get custody.

He didn't want to be separated from them for that long.

But he wouldn't mind being separated from them for tonight. It was a night of celebration.

Speaking of, he saw Shanna walking toward him.

Her little sister had graduated in his class.

Looking at Shanna didn't make him feel the same as he felt when he saw Ellen sitting in the crowd.

She made him feel...he couldn't even explain.

Ellen made him want to be a better person, a bigger person, someone who worked harder, did right, was more compassionate and kind. She brought out the very best in him.

Shanna made him feel edgy. Tempted. Excited in a dangerous way. Like he was walking a tightrope over the edge of Niagara Falls without a net.

It was a thrill but a cheap one.

"Congratulations, farm boy. You got that little piece of paper that says you're free. How does it feel?" Shanna batted her eyes at him and put her hand on his forearm. She squeezed, almost like she was testing it out, to see whether there was anything of substance in his forearm.

He wanted to ask her if there was, but he really didn't care what she thought.

"Feels good," he said simply. She didn't care how he felt. He knew that by now. She cared how she looked when she was beside him.

Ever since he won the football game, it had changed things for him at school. He had been accepted into the popular cliques and invited to the best parties.

"We're having a party at my house later. Not at my house." She rolled her eyes. "In the hollow behind my house. It will have to be late, at least eleven. My parents always go to bed at nine, but just to make sure they're asleep."

She threw a glance over her shoulder, almost as though checking to make sure her parents weren't listening. "We have a keg, and we'll have some dust. It'll be good stuff."

She gave him a smile, and her hands slid up his arm to his bicep. Her fingers curled around it, making him want to pull away but press closer at the same time. She always made him feel like that. He hated it, except he felt like the proverbial moth drawn to the flame. He couldn't seem to pull away.

"If you can make it." Her voice was low and sultry, and it sent shivers down his spine.

She leaned toward him, her shirt low-cut, tempting him to look down. There wouldn't be much left to the imagination if he did.

"Thanks. I'll think about it."

Drugs and alcohol. All the stuff he was supposed to avoid. All the things that got his mom into trouble, all the things that kept her from being a good mom, kept her from being able to support and take care of her family, because she spent all of her money catering to her addictions.

The temptation was there though. To want to do what Shanna wanted him to do. To go where she was, to fly closer to the flame.

Even though he knew the flame destroyed. Just like it had destroyed his mother. Could destroy all his plans, from his chance of making sure that his brothers got the education they needed, and had a solid and stable influence in their life, to his plans of having a job and a solid start in life.

"Don't let me down, Travis. I...have special plans for you. I'm pretty sure you'll be very pleased with what I want to do with you." She looked at him in such a way that he was pretty sure he knew exactly what she wanted to do.

And he wanted it. Absolutely he wanted it. Except, he didn't. Not with Shanna.

In theory anyway. In reality, she was offering, and he wanted to take her up on it.

She pursed her lips and blew him an air kiss before she lowered her lashes and fluttered them, then turned and walked away, her hips swaying, her skirt short, her heels high, her legs long and shapely.

Travis found it hard to swallow. And he almost jumped when Tadgh grabbed a hold of his arm.

"Congratulations, son. I can't tell you how proud I was of you tonight. How wonderful it was to see you up there on that stage, to get that diploma. I know how hard you worked for it. You deserved every second of the spotlight."

Travis laughed, the sound coming out a little higher than he wanted to. "That walk across the stage felt like it took forever. Mostly because I was afraid I was going to trip and take down the principal instead of reaching out and taking my diploma."

"Well, that didn't happen, so you can be grateful for little things, I guess," Tadgh said, his hand clasping Travis's shoulder, making him feel good. Almost like a son.

"Travis, you look so calm and confident, no one would believe for one second that you were afraid of falling," Miss Ashley said from beside her husband. She didn't shake his hand but wrapped her arms around him and gave him a warm, motherly hug. Despite the small bump of her belly.

They were expecting a child in late summer, and Travis was excited and happy for them. And a little jealous. He wished he had been born into a family with love and light and laughter.

As Miss Ashley pulled back, his eyes fell on Ellen.

There was something in her eyes, something that made him think she had seen him talking to Shanna and had known exactly what Shanna had said, what she had invited him to do, or, maybe more accurately, like she knew how tempted he was to take her up on it.

It made him feel ashamed. The same way he would feel if Jesus was standing there looking at him, knowing his thoughts.

That made him desire to be closer to Ellen but, at the same time, made him want to be further away.

Still, she'd been as good a friend as anyone had ever been to him, faithful and true even when he wasn't popular. She'd been kind and never looked down on him or made fun of him because he was poor or because his mother was in jail or drunk somewhere or known as a waste.

People only whispered, but he knew.

Still, Ellen had been steadfast in her friendship. Nothing had shaken her.

"Hey there," he said, reaching out and ruffling her hair the way she hated.

"Hey, farm boy."

From Shanna, it sounded like a put-down, from Ellen, it sounded like a compliment. He loved it when she called him that.

He certainly would never tell her, though.

"You didn't throw up, and you didn't trip, so you did well tonight," she said with a little smile. But still, in her eyes, he read the betrayal. Or, maybe not betrayal, just disappointment.

She had seen him with Shanna.

Not that it mattered. He didn't think about Ellen the same way he thought about Shanna. Shanna was...sultry and beautiful, the kind of woman who caught a man's eye and made him think of hot summer nights and rumpled sheets and made him feel that the consequences of sin for a season would be worth it.

While Ellen, with her childish look, the baby fat around her belly and on her face, just made him think of a warm kitchen, good food, great conversation, and a faithful friend. A faithful, loyal friend.

Far better than sultry nights and sweet, forbidden sin, but as a man, those sultry nights and rumpled sheets were a huge draw.

"Thanks. Just a few years and it'll be your turn. I wish the same for you. No puking and no tripping."

"I'm not worried about it. If I trip, I'll just pick myself up and keep walking. And if I throw up, at least I won't have to worry about anybody trying to sit in my lap."

He laughed. Nothing ruffled her. She would always have an answer for everything.

He stood and talked to Tadgh and Miss Ashley and Ellen for a little bit more. They offered to take him out for ice cream, but he declined, and he did so without looking at Ellen.

He didn't want to be late for the party.

Chapter 23

Ellen stood in the barn, brushing Rosemary, the latest heifer that she'd bottle-fed from a baby.

Changes were always sad. She was starting to recognize that. Even changes that were good, like Uncle Tadgh marrying Aunt Ashley. That was a good change, and it was mostly happy but still sad. Because she had to share Uncle Tadgh now. Of course, she got Aunt Ashley in exchange, but sometimes she still missed the days where it was just her and her uncle and they were buddies together.

Now, with the new little one on the way, her life would change again. She was a little bit sad, sad because she wished she had siblings when she was younger. She missed that. Sad that she'd only have a few years with this one before she was out of the house. Sad that Uncle Tadgh and Aunt Ashley would have someone else to dote on, and she worried that her position in the home would be less than, or maybe they'd forget about her altogether. Maybe they'd think she was in the way.

But mostly, she was sad because Travis had graduated, and he almost certainly wasn't going to be staying around.

Most likely he would find a job somewhere which would pay well, and he'd be off.

Of course, first, tonight, he was going to Shanna's party. Everybody was going to Shanna's party. It was such a huge party, even Ellen had heard about it, although she hadn't been invited to it.

When she'd seen Travis talking to Shanna, and him nodding his head, she figured that he'd just agreed to go.

It made her sad. Then, when her family had gone over and offered him ice cream, and he declined, Ellen had wanted to disappear through the floor. After all, why would he want to go out for ice cream with her family, when he had Shanna waiting for him in the woods in the dark around the campfire with beer and all the things that happened at parties like that.

All the things Ellen would never be good at and would never be interested in any way, except she was, because it would mean being with Travis.

She felt like they were friends. Was pretty sure about that, but she'd known for a while that she liked him more. She'd also known for just as long, or maybe even longer, that he would never like her like he liked Shanna. He thought of her as a kid, ruffled her hair, and sometimes visited her or walked beside her, but never any more than that.

The barn door creaked, and she almost didn't turn around, assuming it was the wind.

But Rosemary lifted her head and mooed, low and soft, like she was saying *hey, how are you?*

It made Ellen turn her head.

Travis stood in the doorway.

"Hey, kid," he said, stepping in and closing the barn door behind him.

"What's the matter? Are you lost?" Ellen asked, and she was rather proud of herself, because while the questions weren't the most polite thing she'd ever said to anyone, they didn't hold any bitterness. Not like she felt in her heart.

She sniffed as he came closer. He smelled like woodsmoke but not like alcohol.

He stopped, standing on the other side of Rosemary, his hands on her back. "I come here all the time. What would make you think I'm lost?"

"I thought you'd be looking for Shanna's party."

"I figured you saw me talking to her. You never miss anything."

"It was kind of hard to miss. Uncle Tadgh and Aunt Ashley did nothing but talk about you all night, and as soon as it was over and we could get up, they made a beeline to you, and the whole time we were walking, you were talking to Shanna."

"Right. Because you don't look at me if you don't have to."

"I never said that."

"You didn't have to."

"You don't know anything." That time, there was anger in her voice. He really didn't. He didn't know anything. Nothing at all.

"What was that for?" he asked, sounding surprised.

"Nothing." She ran the brush down Rosemary's neck, wishing he'd just leave her alone. Her cow was much better company than he ever would be.

"If I don't know anything, maybe you can tell me what I don't know," he said, leaning down like he was trying to catch her eye.

"There's nothing to tell you," she said, feeling moody. Which she hated. She was never moody. She was consistent, and she always did the right thing.

She wasn't being a very good friend right now. But she supposed it was because she was jealous. She'd seen the way Travis looked at Shanna. It wasn't the way he looked at her.

There wasn't any point being mad at Travis because he didn't feel the way she wanted him to. And there was no point in being mad at Shanna because she was doing what she had been brought up to do.

"Ellen?"

"Yeah?"

He just stood and looked at her.

"I like cows better than people. Rosemary's been a good friend."

There she was, being dumb again. Acting like a little kid, talking about how much she loved her cow. Yeah, that was real sexy.

"Ellen?"

"What?"

"Shanna invited me to her party, and I'm not going to deny that I was tempted to go. All for the wrong reasons. So, I walked here, because I can depend on you to make me want to do the right thing. Most of the time."

"Most of the time?"

He didn't say any more, just stared at her, his eyes dark and a little hooded.

The look he gave her made her breath catch in her throat.

"Yeah. Most of the time," he said, softly, like he was thinking. Maybe like his thoughts were surprising him.

"When have I ever encouraged you to do anything other than the right thing?" she asked, a little annoyed that he would accuse her of trying to lead him wrong. She never had. Not ever.

"Right now," he said, his face just a few inches from hers.

"You're here instead of at Shanna's beer party. What's wrong with that?"

She didn't know exactly what was at Shanna's party, but she assumed there'd be bad things there, alcohol for sure, possibly drugs, definitely sex. All things that Travis, if anyone, should know were things he should avoid.

"Maybe being here is more dangerous for me than being at Shanna's party," he murmured.

"I hardly think so."

"You don't?"

"No. There's no drugs, there's no alcohol, there's nothing here that could possibly get you into trouble."

"I could kiss you."

Ellen's eyes flew to his. Her mouth opened. Her intake of air clear in the stillness of the barn.

"But you wouldn't," she finally said, when she could get her mouth to work.

"Not because I don't want to."

"You do?"

"Yeah." He sounded like he couldn't quite believe it.

"Then do it." Her words surprised her.

"You're thirteen, Ellen. I'm eighteen. You know what would happen if I kissed you? You know what would happen to me?"

"But we're friends."

"Now. I know." He ran a hand through his hair, straightening, walking away. Before turning back, leaning over Rosemary, his look intense, his words even more so. "We're friends. You've never been anything but the best friend I could possibly ask for. Faithful to me, steadfast in your support. It didn't matter what I did, you were behind me every step of the way, you fed me, you cared for me, you sent food home for my brothers, and that was when you didn't even have parents yourself."

"I still don't," she said, more sad than she cared to admit.

"Miss Ashley loves you. She loves you like a daughter."

"She has her own child coming."

"That doesn't mean she's going to love you less."

"It doesn't matter."

"You're right. It doesn't. I've never had a friend like you. Never had anyone in my life like you. I don't want to screw up what we have."

"I don't want you to go to jail," she said, lifting her brows like she dared him to contradict that.

He huffed out a laugh. "I don't want to go to jail either. So I guess that makes two of us."

They smiled at each other.

"I like you, Ellen."

"I like you. I always have. I've always admired you, and I like being around you." She paused, then she said, "Travis?"

"What?" he asked, one of his lips pulling back like her words hadn't made him feel any better about himself.

"I wouldn't mind if you kissed me."

His breath came fast, his eyes as dark as she'd ever seen them, his face just inches from hers. "I might not be able to stop. And you're just a kid."

"Are you trying to say that we can't be friends?" she asked, her brows drawing down. She didn't understand. He didn't want to kiss her, or he wanted to. She wasn't sure. Then he talked about what a good friend she was, almost as though he were...saying goodbye.

"I don't want to lose your friendship. But I don't want to ruin it either." He straightened. "It might be best for me to leave."

She stared at him, not wanting him to go, sad and a little scared.

The idea that he might kiss her, that he wanted to, had shaken her whole world. But she wasn't stupid, either. Her uncle wouldn't be happy about that, and Travis was right anyway. He could get in a lot of trouble. She absolutely didn't want that for him. Not because of her.

It would be one thing if he went to Shanna's party and got in trouble, that would break her heart, but if he kissed her and got in trouble, that would be on her, and she would hate herself for it.

She would also hate herself if he kissed her but was thinking of Shanna.

"Do you mind if I write to you?" he asked.

"You're leaving?"

"I had a couple of job offers. I wasn't going to take them, but after tonight, I think that would be the best thing. But...I want to write."

"Of course. But...don't leave. You don't have to leave." She knew her voice sounded panicked, but she couldn't help it. She didn't want him to go anywhere. She looked forward to seeing him, almost every day.

"Ford Hansen has made me a couple of offers, things that will give me a good start in life, not only help make money, but learn to handle a business, and maybe even start my own."

"All right," Ellen said faintly, not really meaning it, but what else could she do? Beg him not to go? Why would she do that if Ford

Hansen was actually going to help him get a job and mentor him? She'd be foolish to not encourage that. "I'd love it if you'd write to me. Make sure you include your address, and I'll write back. I'll answer every letter."

"I know you will." He ran another hand through his hair. Agitated. "I don't have any right to ask this, but...wait for me."

"Where? What do you mean?" She looked around, thinking he was going to leave and come back. Of course she would wait for him if he were coming back tonight, although her uncle might have something to say about her being out past midnight. Normally he didn't care if she was out in the barn till all hours, but she was never out any later than that. Not just because she had to get up early in the morning, but she didn't like the way she felt when she didn't get enough sleep.

"No. I mean..." He swallowed, looking down, then looking back into her eyes. "I mean...that kiss. The one that I'm not getting tonight. I... I wanted it, but I'll wait for it. Years. That's what it's going to take. But I was hoping you'd wait for me."

"Of course," she whispered.

"If you can't wait, if you find someone better, I understand. I'm...not much. Not much potential, not much to look at, not much of anything."

"That's not true. You're strong and brave and determined. Look at what you've done despite your mom." Then she thought about his brothers. "You're leaving your brothers?"

"I know your uncle will look after them, the same way he looked after me. I know you'll befriend them, the same way you befriended me. I just hope you...feel a little different about me than you feel about them."

"There's no one that compares to you. Not to me. Not anywhere. And there never will be." She spoke with confidence, believing every word.

"The years have a way of changing people. Maybe as you grow, you'll see that I'm not really what you think. That I am just...nothing."

"That will never happen," she said, almost angry.

"We'll see. You said you'd wait, and I know you'll keep your word."

"You can count on it."

"I might see you around. But, then again, it might be better that I don't."

"I can't imagine it would be."

"You promised you'd write. Take care, Ellen." With that, he turned and didn't look back as he walked out the barn door, closing it behind him.

Ellen, her hands on Rosemary, stood and stared at the barn door for a long time before she laid her head down on the back of her cow and let her tears drip silently into her fur.

Chapter 24

"It's hard to believe that just a month ago there was four feet of snow on the ground."

Piper sat on the back porch beside her husband, her hand in his, enjoying the dark beauty of a North Dakota summer night.

"I know. It melted fast, then we had mud, then dust. North Dakota is nothing but a land of extremes."

"I love it."

"Me too. It grows the best kind of woman."

"You're such a charmer." She batted her eyes at him, her stomach doing a small loop, which was the only sign of how nervous she was. "I can't believe it was just a month ago that you started this addition. And, it's finished, down to the very lovely porch, perfect for enjoying a summer night."

"I thought of you the whole time I was building it," he said and his words sounded simple, but they held all the love and care he'd shown her since the day he came.

"I wish I could have helped you more."

"I love that you broke your foot and couldn't work, because I loved having you beside me while I did it. Those are memories I'll look back on, every time I think of building this, as we live in it, as we raise our family here."

She smiled, laying her head on his shoulder, her stomach still unsettled, but her heart happy. Today they'd finished their new bedroom and had moved into it. Tonight they'd have their own room, just the two of them, and a door.

"I was expecting to be a lot more sore than what I am," he said, his arm curling down beside her, holding her close.

"This new boot is great, but I was probably on my foot a little more than I should have been and I can feel it throbbing some."

"I should have made you rest more."

"I wanted to get it done."

"Me too."

His voice held humor, but there was also an undercurrent of anticipation.

It gave her the courage to say, "I've been looking forward to tonight."

"It's good to hear you say that. I wondered."

"I can't believe you did. I mean, I tried not to be a love-sick teenager, but that's what this last month has felt like."

He laughed. "You and me, both." His hand rubbed her arm. "But, I guess, unlike my teen years, I enjoyed the anticipation. The knowledge that there didn't need to be any kind of rush. That I wasn't going to lose you, that you weren't going to lose interest, that, no matter how long it took, or what happened, we'd be together through it all. I don't recall feeling that secure in a relationship in my life before."

"That's so mature."

"You don't feel the same?"

"I feel secure in our relationship, sure. But...I wasn't nearly so patient in waiting for us to have our own room. Privacy." She felt like she could tell him anything. "I'm nervous. But excited."

"That sums up my feelings, too."

"As pretty as the night is, I'm tired of waiting."

He laughed again. "Me, too."

"So...are you ready to go to bed?" She turned her face up and kissed the side of his neck.

"I thought you'd never ask."

She smiled against his skin, kissing him once more before she stood with her husband and walked into their new addition together, the faint oink of a settling piglet out in the shed following them inside.

Enjoy this preview of *Just a Cowboy's Princess,* just for you!

Just A Cowboy's Princess

Chapter 1

T he paparazzi had arrived.

Princess Kennedy Weaver-Payne, known as Kenni to her family and friends, froze on the sidewalk as three cars pulled up to the diner in Sweet Water, catty-corner across the street from where she was. People pouring out of all four doors, cameras around their necks, phones in hand, press badges lying like bull's-eyes on lanyards against their chests.

Thankfully they didn't glance her way. Possibly it was because of the short brown hair, or maybe the cheap five-dollar department store sunglasses, or maybe it was the prairie skirt and peasant blouse she wore.

Hardly the long blonde locks they were used to seeing, perfectly coiffured, the designer suits, and expensive matching pumps.

An outfit like she normally wore would draw their eye immediately but would definitely make her look out of place in this small town.

Regardless, the second-to-last person paused on the sidewalk, looking up at the sky before slowly turning.

Kenni's eyes opened wide, and her heart beat hard.

While she felt like her new look was different enough from her old one that she probably wouldn't be recognized, her brother would kill her if he knew she just stood on the sidewalk while the paparazzi poured out around her.

Seeing the big shaggy cow that her brother had told her was Sweet Water's own matchmaking steer, which had caused Kenni to roll her eyes at the antics small towns would go to in order to pull in tourism dollars, just up the street from where she stood, she took five big strides and ducked down behind it.

It had been standing in the same spot since she arrived with her brother in his pickup, contentedly chewing its cud, with its eyes half closed, looking like it had nothing better in the world to do than stand along the sidewalk in Sweet Water and soak up the summer sun.

Kenni had been a little jealous.

Billy, that's what Zeke, her brother, had said the steer's name was, was the town celebrity, and yet he could stand on the sidewalk in peace, no one criticizing his every move, critiquing his outfit, his mannerism, whether he smiled or didn't smile, and whether it was the right time to smile, or, worse than that, determining that it was somehow Billy's fault that his spouse had cheated on him.

The way Kenni's had cheated on her.

Pain went through her, not so much because she had been madly in love with her husband. But because she had trusted him, and his betrayal cut deep.

Taking a deep breath that shook as it entered her body, she tried to focus on the moment at hand, bending over and making sure that her entire body was hidden behind the steer, who hadn't seemed to notice that anything had changed in his life, or maybe he was just used to people crouching down behind him trying to hide themselves from the paparazzi that normally descended upon the small town.

Hardly.

Maybe she shouldn't have come. It seemed like such a quaint town. So old fashioned almost, and friendly. She hated to ruin those vibes with the sharks that circled the water around her, sensing blood and wanting to get a part of the kill.

"Excuse me. I'm going to assume that you're Kenni," a deep voice said above her.

If she hadn't been bent over, trying to hide herself behind the steer's body, obviously not acting like a normal person, she might have described the voice as...sexy.

Definitely the kind of voice that sent all the good shivers down her backbone and made her fingertips tingle.

One that actually sounded familiar.

Probably because she'd heard it shouting at her at some point to turn around so he could get a better picture.

The paparazzi had found her.

She reminded herself just in time not to move, even as her brain was saying that the paparazzi did not call her Kenni.

She was Princess Kennedy, and her name had never been shortened from the time Isaac had first introduced her to his world, until she had stepped out of it just a couple of months ago.

She tilted her head, maybe against her better judgment, to get a better look at the man who had come over and had just...crouched down beside her.

He had crouched.

He wore a T-shirt, which stretched over his shoulders, his brown neck showing that he spent time in the sun and similar brown arms that were roped with muscle.

Worn blue jeans.

Not exactly clothes the paparazzi usually wore when they chased her.

Plus, he had a cowboy hat pulled low over his eyes, like he used it to shade his face and not to make himself look good.

There was something familiar about the angle of his jaw.

"It's a risky thing to make assumptions," she finally said, not forgetting, even in her nervousness and insecurity, to use anything other than her most cultured voice.

"You don't sound like the Kenni I knew," the man said with a little bit of a grin.

"Who are you?" she asked, and though she might be crouching behind a cow, she wasn't going to beat around the bush.

Not that there were any bushes in sight.

"It was a long time ago. Your brother's in there dealing with the bottom-feeders, and he sent me out here to rescue you. But he forgot to hand me his keys, and my truck is parked behind the diner. So, we're going to have to figure out how to get you from here to there and make it look like you're supposed to be with me."

"You don't think they're gonna leave?" she asked, wanting to peek around the steer but knowing she shouldn't.

"They have your brother. They think you're with him. And they're not far off from the truth. Except, if I can get you out of here, you won't be."

"What makes you think I should go with you?"

"I'm a buddy of your brother's from the Air Force."

That was all he needed to say. She knew how much Zeke thought of his Air Force cronies. She also knew the code the men shared would keep them from doing anything to harm her.

Plus, while Zeke probably had a few guys who didn't like him, everyone did, they wouldn't be hanging out in Sweet Water. This man had come to keep her safe, and if there was any danger in the town itself, he would have said something.

The man's eyes were shadowed, but there was a hint of a smile around his lips as he looked at her, probably knowing that was all he had to say in order to make her trust him.

The man pulled a necklace out from around his neck, unhooking it and allowing something to drop in his hand.

"Do me a favor, take this ring and put it on your ring finger, and I'm gonna put my arm around you, and we're going to laugh together, like we're a couple. Princess Kennedy Weaver-Payne is not laughing with and married to someone else. Hopefully, anyone who glances in our direction will dismiss us as uninteresting. That should get us across the street and behind the diner to my pickup."

"What's plan B?" she asked, even as she took the ring he gave her and slid it onto the ring finger of her left hand. It was a little loose, but it would work.

"We depend on your disguise. Which, I have to say, is not that good. I'd recognize your nose anywhere."

"My nose?"

"I always had a thing for noses."

"Baker Lawrence?"

She couldn't believe it. Her brother's best friend, their neighbor in the small Virginia town they grew up in, and her childhood crush.

He was only two years older than she was, but she thought he'd hung the moon and painted the sunrises too.

She would never have told her husband, but she occasionally still dreamed about him. Not that she wanted to, just that she'd been so stuck on him for so many years.

He had been her first kiss.

"I'm not sure what that says about me that I mention my nose issue and you instantly recognize me."

"Maybe if you weren't wearing that ridiculous cowboy hat, I would have recognized you just by looking at you."

"Hmm. I'm not sure I want to be married to someone who thinks my hat is ridiculous."

"I'm not the one who asked you to marry me."

"I don't think I asked. I just gave you a ring and told you to pretend for a little bit."

"I guess it doesn't really matter what I think about your hat, since you hate my nose so much."

"I never said I hated your nose. Just that I recognized it." He glanced around the body of the steer, giving a jerk of his chin that she assumed meant the coast was clear.

He straightened, standing so the upper half of his body was visible to the paparazzi over the back of the steer who still stood in front of them.

She slowly followed him up. A lot more cautious, just because she knew how unshakable the paparazzi could be.

Of course, they had played in her favor at times as well. And they had come down squarely on her side when Isaac had cheated. Of course, Isaac was still the heir to the throne, and he would eventually be exonerated while she would fade into oblivion.

She had to admit she wouldn't mind it. The last ten years of constantly being in the eye of the world, her every move scrutinized, never knowing who she could trust, who would sell their soul, and her secrets, for whatever price the paparazzi was willing to pay, had taken a huge toll on her.

The worst, the very worst, was that she hadn't known who she could trust.

In this small town, she wanted to think that problem was over, but she wasn't entirely sure.

Regardless, she knew she could trust Baker. It was a good feeling.

Trying to do everything on her own had been exhausting.

"What in the world made you think I hated your nose?" Baker said as he looked down on her, waiting for her to straighten her clothes and brush her skirt off, just in case she picked up any dirt from the sidewalk.

"You always make fun of it."

"I never made fun of it. I always said it made you look aristocratic. Which was basically almost like fortune-telling since you ended up marrying an aristocrat."

"The biggest mistake of my life," she couldn't help but mutter.

"Sorry," Baker said, the teasing note out of his voice and true contrition entering it.

She appreciated that he felt bad for bringing it up, but she didn't want anyone to have to walk on eggshells around her. She wanted to be able to 'fess up to the mistakes she had made and not allow them to get her down.

Of course, the dissolution of the marriage she expected to last for a lifetime might take more than a few months to get over.

The pain was still fresh. The betrayal still cut deep. Her ability to trust might never recover.

After all, Isaac had been known as a very straightlaced and somewhat boring man who followed the rules. Did what he was told. Never stepped a foot out of line.

What had been so terrible about her that had made him feel like he couldn't stay in his marriage for whatever it was he needed from a woman?

That had been the question on everyone's mind, and she had read it more than once in the papers. And online.

Questioning whether she had been an absolute hag behind closed doors. Hag, nag, witch—she had all the names thrown at her. And it had finally gotten to her, how everyone thought it was her fault.

"All right, give me your hand, and then see if you can't put those latent acting skills to use."

"Latent acting skills?" she asked, scrunching her brows down, as she put her hand into his.

Despite the heat of the day, her fingers were cool, and she welcomed the warmth of his rough skin. The tingles that his voice had elicited multiplied as her fingers lay in his.

Thankful for her dark shades, she closed her eyes and looked away, ostensibly toward the diner where the vehicles that had spit out the paparazzi were still parked, squatting there as though claiming the ground for their own.

"Ready?"

"I don't understand what you said about my acting skills, but of course. I'm ready."

"You're going to have to act like you like me. Or at least, like you think I'm funny."

"I do like you. And I do think you're funny. Although it's been a long time, and I suppose you changed since I last spoke with you."

"That's news to me. I didn't think you liked me at all, and I really didn't think you thought I was funny. All of these compliments at one time are going to give a guy a big head."

"That's good. Maybe your hat will start fitting."

He barked out a laugh, and she smiled.

"If you don't like it, I can lose it," he said, taking his hat off and slapping his leg with it.

His hair was a little shorter than he'd worn it in high school, but his nose was exactly the same. A strong Roman nose that she'd teased him about just as much as he'd teased her about her aristocratic nose.

It was a little crooked, and he always claimed it was because his parents dropped him on his head when he was a baby.

She figured he probably fell down and hit it somewhere, but she'd never heard the story, if there even was one.

"I see your nose is still crooked," she murmured as they stepped around the steer.

"The one imperfect thing on my face, and she always zeroes in on it," he said, rather fatalistically.

"All right. Neutral territory. My brother said that steer is a matchmaking steer. I have to disagree, and I would say that he is more like a really good hiding spot."

"Actually, I'd need two hands to tell you all the couples in town that steer had a part in bringing together."

"Oh, so now you're on the tourism board in Sweet Water?" she asked with a raised brow.

He laughed and shook his head. "I know. We both come from small towns, and we know how they grasp at everything trying to get people to see their virtues. But I'm not kidding about this."

"Well, I have to say I'm unimpressed, not to mention, if he's going to be trying to matchmake me, he's going to be sadly disappointed."

"I don't know about that. We spent about two minutes together behind him, and now we're married." He lifted up the hand he held, the one with the ring on it, and she laughed. "Admit it. I'm right."

"It's a fake marriage. Just until we get across the street. After that, I'm gone."

She didn't mean that. She didn't take marriage vows so lightly. She couldn't even believe she was joking about it now. Especially after Isaac had played so fast and loose with his.

The sad thing was, she probably would have taken him back. Except he didn't want her. He wanted to be with the other woman.

She pushed those thoughts out of her head. She couldn't heal if all she did was pick her wounds open every time the thoughts came into her mind.

"Oh no," Baker said, causing her to pause and look up at him. He sounded truly horrified.

"What?"

"It's Miss April. And...it looks like she has her arm around one of the paparazzi."

Pick up your copy of *Just a Cowboy's Princess* by Jessie Gussman today!

A Gift from Jessie

View this code through your smart phone camera to be taken to a page where you can download a FREE ebook when you sign up to get updates from Jessie Gussman! Find out why people say, "Jessie's is the only newsletter I open and read" and "You make my day brighter. Love, love, love reading your newsletters. I don't know where you find time to write books. You are so busy living life. A true blessing." and "I know from now on that I can't be drinking my morning coffee while reading your newsletter – I laughed so hard I sprayed it out all over the table!"

Claim your free book from Jessie!

Escape to more faith-filled romance series by Jessie Gussman!

The Complete Sweet Water, North Dakota Reading Order:

Series One: Sweet Water Ranch Western Cowboy Romance (11 book series)

Series Two: Coming Home to North Dakota (12 book series)

Series Three: Flyboys of Sweet Briar Ranch in North Dakota (13 book series)

Series Four: Sweet View Ranch Western Cowboy Romance (10 book series)

Spinoffs and More! Additional Series You'll Love:

Jessie's First Series: Sweet Haven Farm (4 book series)

Small-Town Romance: The Baxter Boys (5 book series)

Bad-Boy Sweet Romance: Richmond Rebels Sweet Romance (3 book series)

Sweet Water Spinoff: Cowboy Crossing (9 book series)

Holiday Romance: Cowboy Mountain Christmas (6 book series)

Small Town Romantic Comedy: Good Grief, Idaho (5 book series)

True Stories from Jessie's Farm: Stories from Jessie Gussman's Newsletter (3 book series)

Reader-Favorite! Sweet Beach Romance: Blueberry Beach (8 book series)

Cowboy Mountain Christmas Spinoff: A Heartland Cowboy Christmas (9 book series)

Blueberry Beach Spinoff: Strawberry Sands (10 book series)

Printed in the USA
CPSIA information can be obtained
at www.ICGtesting.com
LVHW011226270324
775600LV00011B/385

9 781953 066817